A PLACE CALLED *Happiness*

DIANA ANYANGO

Diana Anyango

First Published in Great Britain in 2020 by
LOVE AFRICA PRESS
103 Reaver House, 12 East Street, Epsom KT17 1HX
www.loveafricapress.com

ISBN: 978-1-914226-01-4
Also available as ebook

Blurb

Abandoned in an orphanage as a child, Geraldine Aketch's scars are deep and still hurting. When the architect of her pain, her mother, crawls back seeking forgiveness, Geraldine is not ready to let her into her life and leaves home.

Brandon Odhiambo is a broken man. His wife ran off with his best friend and he must stay strong to take care of his daughter. Love is the last thing on his mind. Until he meets Geraldine.

Desire so strong brews between them. But their past lives intrude, and love is put to the test. Can they find a place called happiness, together?

Acknowledgements

I would like to thank God for the gift of writing and life.

I would like to acknowledge my mentor Dr. David Mulwa for his unwavering faith in my writing. I remember him telling 'Keep writing' when I could not get any publisher for my book and I was feeling dejected. I couldn't have done it without you.

I want to appreciate my friends Bwari and Ephy for believing in me and my works way back then.

I would like to appreciate my Mom, Beatrice Awiti, for always reading my books and encouraging me.

My Grandpa, John Awiti, was very supportive of my writing dream, thank you so much.

This journey wouldn't have been a success without Love Africa Press. Thank you very much Kiru Taye for turning my dream into a beautiful reality.

Zee Monodee, you are simply the best editor, polishing the story and making it shine.

The book is dedicated to my daughter, Mariallison Akinyi, who renewed my hope in finding true love.

Diana Anyango

Chapter One

Gera Aketch's footsteps trudged along the Kisumu-Kakamega road, her whole body tired and sweating from the afternoon sun. She did not even have an exact destination in mind, but one thing was for sure, she was not going back home. Her mother and sister had made it clear that they wanted nothing to do with her. After all, she was twenty-one years old and could fend for herself, right?

In a way, this brought relief, that no one was expecting anything from her, but in some other way, it also made her lonely, with no shoulder to lean on. Then again, she was used to being alone. She even wondered if it was her fate to always be alone—a very depressing thought, which only made her feel sorry for herself. She shrugged and continued walking.

When she reached Mamboleo Estate, she felt too tired and hungry to move a further step, but this also made her realize she was desperately in need of food and a place to rest. The passers-by kept glancing at her suspiciously, and she momentarily forgot about fatigue and hunger. Her white floral dress looked tattered, in dire need of washing. Her feet were covered with dust, and she wore red slippers on one foot and a blue one on the other. What!

After the confrontation with her mother earlier in the morning, she had been in such a hurry to leave that she had not bothered to take care of her looks. She had wanted nothing more than to distance herself from her so-called home in Rongo as soon as possible. Home was no longer a safe haven to shield her from the dangers of the world. The orphanage had felt more like home than the *mabati* house her mother now lived in.

Deep inside, she knew that home was more than just a structure. A home constituted of people who cared for and loved one another. Her mother's cold eyes held no warmth or even love—she'd realized the woman wasn't capable of loving anybody else but herself.

Gera wanted fun, happiness, and love. She had once read about that place called happiness, and she hoped with the whole of her heart that she was going to find it. Mama Jane from the orphanage had also believed in that place where everything was going to be perfect with the world.

The rumbling of her stomach reminded her to deal with first things first. At the moment, her hunger took priority. The problem was, there was no food in the vicinity, unless she climbed the mango tree just a stone's throw away. The tree had juicy fruit, and she was already salivating. It was immodest for a girl to go on climbing trees, but to Hell with modesty. Desperate situations called for desperate measures.

She freed herself of her slippers and started her climb, then accidentally stepped on a feeble branch and almost lost her grip. Her poor heart raced, but the loud rumbling of her stomach could not allow her to surrender. *One more step*, she convinced herself, and she would be at her target—a big, yellow mango.

She stretched her hand some more and plucked it, munched on the fruit ferociously, drawing in as much juice as she could. She did not mind that it had not been washed; after all, germs could wait. Right now, she was dealing with her state of emergency. She ate more than five mangoes before she could even start to get satisfied.

She was onto the seventh one when she had this sudden feeling of someone watching her. The thing was, she did not know whether this inkling had been concealed by hunger and she had been watched for a while. She became paranoid all of a sudden, looked about her with keen interest, taking in the details of her surroundings for the first time. Unfortunately, she could not see anyone, and that only worried her more.

Someone cleared his throat from below the tree, and she quickly looked down. Why had she not thought of that? Blame it on the mango. She smiled when she remembered the pastor preaching about God hiding things by putting them close to us.

Under the tree, she saw what some girls would call a tall, dark, and handsome man. He wore a very expensive dark suit with a white button-down shirt, no tie, and the first four buttons of his shirt were open, revealing some dark chest hair. On the right hand, he held the coat to his suit.

When their eyes met, he smiled knowingly at her. Gera felt all the blood rushing away from her head. Just one look and a smile from a handsome man, and she got dizzy—what was wrong with her?

***

Brandon Odhiambo had been standing there for a long moment, wondering what on Earth somebody was doing on his mango tree. He did not have much to do in the office today and had therefore decided to return home to rest, only to spot someone in the branches.

At first, he had thought it was the mischievious neighbors' children. As he'd moved closer to get a clearer view, he'd been astonished to find that the culprit was an adult. To add further intrigue to the mystery, it was a lady. He could not have been more amused—not every day that you came home from work to find a lady on your tree.

"What are you staring at?" she shouted from up there.

He thought he heard a tremor in her voice. Was she scared? She was a vulnerable woman, and here he was, a man sent to come and save the damsel from her distress. He was going to be the knight in a shining armor, or so he thought.

On the other hand, he was answering her question in his head—she looked at him pointedly. Why could he *not* stare? She was tall, about five-foot-eight, and her smooth, dark skin reminded him of a bar of chocolate. Her dress was riding high on her thighs, exposing thick flesh, and he swallowed the lump that had formed in his throat. Her nipples were also poking at her dress, standing tall. She was a beautiful girl.

No, not a girl, he corrected himself. This was a beautiful woman.

"You are on my land, young lady, and on my tree, if I may remind you," he told her, trying to maintain a no-nonsense tone and failing miserably, since he couldn't contain his smile. There was just something sexy about a woman on top of a tree. Maybe because it defied what was considered normal. It was out of the ordinary—extraordinaire.

"Okay, so what if I am on your land and on your tree? What are you going to do about it?" she retorted, not the least scared, it appeared.

This surprised him. In place of that tremor in her voice, he heard a tough, defiant tone. The vulnerable woman had disappeared just as she had appeared. This woman's neck had stretched high, her eyes glittering with courage and stubbornness. She seemed perfectly capable of taking care of herself, not in need of a knight. This intrigued him even more. He did not know which one of the two he liked more: the vulnerable woman, or Miss Independent. He was yet to find out.

"I could sue you for trespass, you know?" he went on, wanting to have a spar with this war-hungry woman.

She did not seem moved by his words at all.

"I could also sue you for sexual harassment! Go ahead and call the police, it would be my pleasure to accompany them," she retorted.

He was amazed. This girl had a sharp tongue, and he really admired her courage.

On second thought, he was no longer interested in being the knight in shining armor. He liked this fire-spitting woman more. He, too, was stubborn and liked having his own way. He had finally found his match and was suddenly interested.

Ooh. Sexual harassment! He had not committed any sexual harassment offence. He was just a man responding to nature. With a woman this curvaceous, which man in his right senses would not be tempted to stare longer than was considered morally acceptable?

***

When the man did not respond, only stared more, Gera broke eye contact first and glanced away. No one had ever looked at her like that, as if he were undressing her, yet her clothes still clung perfectly to her body.

Time to go. They could talk the whole day, it seemed, good company for each other. If she was to find shelter in good time, she had better get moving.

It was then that she realized she was very high on top of the tree. The problem was that she did not know how to get down now. She was damned if she was going to ask for help from him, especially after posing as Miss Independent.

She did not have any doubt in her mind that he could help her down effortlessly. With a torso like this one and the able, muscular arms, she would be feather weight in his grip. She particularly liked his broad chest. It seemed powerful enough to shield her from the harshness of the world. And only God knew how much she wanted a safe harbor.

She regretfully dragged herself out of the dreamy land and back to reality.

"Owner of the land and tree, I am climbing down and off your land before you can bat an eye," she told him, plastering a smile on her face.

She started climbing down more carefully, not wanting to parade her fundamentals around this man, *especially* this man. After the ogling he had done, she was not in the mood to give body to his imagination.

He just nodded—seemed to her in disbelief. But damn, this was hard to do. The fact that she was also holding her dress as she climbed made it almost impossible to get down.

She was doing quite well with her descent until she touched something warm and rough. She gasped in terror and quickly withdrew her hand. Her first thought was that it was a snake, only to find a fat, brown chameleon. She always saw chameleons, but not at this close range. The animal looked ugly, with big, protruding, round eyes staring at her. She grew very afraid it was going to charge at her.

Given the stories she had heard that once a chameleon sticks on you, there was no way of getting it off, and only thunder and lightning could scare it away, she peered up. A look at the clouds revealed no sign of rain. How could she have been so stupid? Where had she been looking at that she had not seen the chameleon beforehand?

But playing blame games with herself was not going to save her now, she concluded. Plus, the chameleon had camouflaged to the color of the tree, and she had also been keen on holding her dress. She did not know whether to scream or jump. Screaming would have been of no consequence while jumping was only going to break her legs.

But wait. The man!

"Help me, you moron! Can't you see I'm in trouble?" she cried out.

She did not like being in a situation like this one, helpless. Now, she had no option but to ask for his help. But one thing was for sure, she was not going to beg.

"Oh, miss, I do not think I can," he said, smiling his drop-dead smile as if just to annoy her.

And he succeeded. The man thought that he was some god and without him, she could not get down the tree. Well, he was yet to meet this lady from the lakeside. She was going to show him that she was made of tougher stuff. She was not like some timid girls he probably encountered every day.

She looked at the chameleon once more, and to her chagrin, it had not moved even an inch from her. It was still staring at her with those big compound eyes. She moved her hand, and the chameleon also moved some more towards her. She trembled in fear. Where was that tougher stuff right now? Maybe it had been wrong putting up that façade of courage that she did not feel right now. But what was a girl to do?

"All you have to do is ask for help. But it is up to you. It's not like I'm the one on top of a tree within a spitting distance of chameleon," he advised her.

The chameleon came charging at her before she could utter a reply. She had no option but to jump.

The man seemed to respond purely on adrenaline. He dove to break her fall, and her weight made them tumble down beneath the tree. This sent the chameleon flying to the nearby thicket.

It took her a while to come to, and when she did, she found herself atop the stranger. It then hit her that she had not broken even a bone because he had helped her. She was safe and sound.

She then decided to put her pride aside and focus on her knight. When she looked into his face, she found him watching her keenly. What was wrong with this man and him ogling her? Did he know what that did to her? Maybe he knew, and that's why he kept at it.

She was about to reprimand him when she saw his blood-soaked shirt on the right shoulder. For once, she was humbled. She had been rude to this man just moments ago, this stranger who had come to her rescue. He was injured because of her. Just how many wrongs could a woman commit in a day? She grew utterly ashamed.

***

Brandon had a bleeding shoulder, but that somehow did not bother him at the moment. It was the effect of this girl on top of him. He had never felt a fit so right in a very long time. Since Jackie—Shit!

Why did Jackie have such wrong timing of popping into his head? He had to admit that he had kissed so many girls, a number he had lost track of, not that he was counting, yet none of those had felt this right.

"What are you ogling at?"

He just chuckled to himself. This girl was a lot to handle, he had to agree. She then seemed to realize she was still on top of him—a very compromising position. She slowly got up, trying to feel if she had injured any body part. She looked fine, though. He was disappointed when she moved away from him, but there was nothing he could do about it. It had been good while it lasted.

He tried to sit up, but the pain proved too much, and he had to lie on his back again.

"Let me help you, please," she urged, already moving closer to help him.

"I can take care of myself, don't worry. You can get on your way to wherever you were going to," he retorted.

He was not an invalid. He was a man from South Nyanza, and according to the culture, a man was supposed to be the protector and not the casualty. His ego could not allow him to accept help from her. He was supposed to be her knight and not the other way round.

"I can take care of myself," she mimicked, and he had to laugh.

She just had a way of getting onto his nerves. She smiled sweetly at him, and he discovered just how beautiful she was. Her smile could lighten up a gloomy day.

"This is entirely my fault. I would like to help you so as to clear my conscience," she said at last.

"Yes, Miss Nurse," he told her, letting her off the hook.

He could have gone on giving her hard time, but she seemed very tired. He wondered where she had come from, where she was headed to, and what she had done to make her so exhausted. He dared not ask.

She held his left arm and helped him to a sitting position, then onto his feet.

"Thank you," he mumbled. His shoulder was stinging like hell. He motioned towards a magnificent black gate.

When he rang the bell, the watchman quickly came to open it, horrified when he saw the blood-soaked shirt, but Brandon quickly assured him it was nothing serious.

As they went in, her eyes could not help but wander, and he understood why. The house was painted white and had red roofing. The compound had beautiful, multicoloured foliage consisting of red roses, yellow, white, and pink flowers. The green, well-maintained grass just added to the beauty of the place. A narrow pavement wound around the house.

If he dared say so, it did look rather spectacular.

***

Gera had never seen such a beautiful house. This felt like home. It beckoned to her. For a moment, she wondered whether this was that place called happiness.

The man cleared his throat, interrupting her thoughts.

"I take it you like my home," he commented.

She just shrugged, like it was nothing, then proceeded with him to the front door. He got his keys from his pocket and unlocked the door. A sweet, flowery scent wafted in the air as they went into the house which was very cool. An L-shaped red leather seat in the living room only went further to convince her that this was a very rich man. This house was Heaven on Earth.

She had to lead him to his room and therefore did not have time to look around. Maybe on her way out. His bedroom was the epitome of the house for her. A king-size, four-poster bed occupied the center of the room. On the wall, beautiful pictures of dolphins covered one side to the other with the blue background. The floor had a soft maroon carpet which felt heavenly under the feet.

She helped him onto the bed and then knelt down to help him remove his shoes. Once he was safely on the mattress, she went in search of the bathroom. She saw a door and made an intelligent guess that it must lead to the bathroom, and she was right.

The space had a big white bathtub, and she felt she needed a bath badly—she reeked of sweat and dust. On the floor were white tiles. She took a small basin and half-filled it with hot water. No sooner had she turned to go back to the bedroom than she found herself face to face with him. The water sloshed onto her dress, and she cursed under her breath.

"Aren't you supposed to be lying down?" she asked, and hated that she sounded like his mother. But this man was just difficult.

"I just thought you needed help finding your way around the house," he said, leaning more onto the doorpost.

"Okay, then, let's go," she told him, helping him back into the bedroom.

When his back hit the bed, she started unbuttoning his shirt so as to attend to his injury.

"What are you doing?" he asked.

"What does it seem like I'm doing? You think I want to rape you?" she asked, getting angry without meaning to.

"I had not thought of that. If we are to go towards that direction, I like to engage in consensual sex," he said under his breath, as if knowing that was going to make her angrier.

Anger did indeed get the better part of her, and she yanked off the shirt, hurting his shoulder a second time. But this time, she was not sorry. He writhed in pain, and she smiled, knowing now they were even. Mama Jane would have not been very proud of her right now, but the man was so annoying.

"I bet you have learnt your lesson. We can now get down to business," she told him and liked the rage she saw in his eyes. She knew vengeance was nigh, yet it seemed they brought the worst in each other.

Since she had been a scout at Nyakach Girls' High School, she had ample knowledge of how to dress injuries. She dipped the cloth into the basin containing warm water mixed with Dettol then gently wiped around the cut, being careful not to hurt him.

The first time the cloth came into contact with his cut, he groaned in pain that however seemed to subside after a while. The second time he groaned, she quickly looked into his face and saw his eyes darken, his jaws clenching and unclenching.

"Am I rough?" she asked softly, afraid that she had hurt him.

He shook his head, and whatever she had seen in his eyes disappeared, so that for a moment, she wondered if she had imagined it.

"What's your name?" he asked, watching her intently.

"Geraldine Aketch, although my friends call me Gera," she said, smiling.

"I am Brandon Odhiambo. It's a pleasure to know you, Gera."

"It's a pleasure to know you, too."

Chapter Two

When Gera had finished dressing the cut, she gave him painkillers to relieve the pain. It seemed the drugs were taking their toll on him because he started drifting off to sleep. In no time, he was sound asleep.

He was even more handsome in his sleep, she realized. She now had time to properly look at that chest she had been yearning to check out. She could have looked at it when she was dressing his shoulder, but she'd not dared. She hadn't wanted him to know that his bare chest could make her go ga-ga. The expanse was broader than it had seemed with his shirt on. He had six packs, a clear indication that he worked out.

She felt like touching him just to know how it felt. With her mind set, she stretched her hands, but before she could touch him, he shifted a bit. She quickly withdrew her hand and sat upright. What had she been thinking? When he resumed his even breathing, relief flooded her.

There was nothing left for her to do here. She was still debating whether to leave or stay. For one, it was not polite to leave without telling him. Secondly, she did not want to wake him because he seemed too peaceful to be disturbed. Finally, she decided to stay.

She was tired of just sitting around watching this beau sleep lest she try something stupid. She re-entered the sitting room, wanting to know more about this man. Was he married? Did he have children? For some strange reasons, the idea of him being married did not appeal to her. She did not know why and did not want to explore the possibilities of that thought.

She saw a family picture and moved foward to have a closer look at it. It showed three people: the man dressed in a well-fitting white suit, a white button-down shirt, and a black bow tie, a girl of about ten years dressed in a pink lacy dress, and a very beautiful woman in a shimmery, long, black dress.

Gera looked at the picture keenly. The man was looking into the woman's eyes lovingly, holding her at the small of the back. The woman was smiling up at him like they were sharing their own private joke. The young girl grinned at the camera happily.

That must be his wife and their child. She was disappointed. How she had wished he was a bachelor. So that ...? She could not believe she was thinking about the possibility of something brewing between them.

It was obvious that he was an influential man, and the wife was very elegant. Gera looked down at her dirty clothes, dusty feet, and pitied herself. The man had everything. What could he possibly need her for?

She heard the front door opening and feared it was the wife. She was still forming some form of explanation in her head when she saw the young girl, who was even prettier in person. She wore a red and white checked uniform, with a white collar. Gera quickly read the badge as Arya Primary School. She had very long hair which she held at the back with a red hair band.

The girl extended her hand in greeting. "Good evening. I am Loiser Odhiambo."

"Good evening, Loiser. I am Geraldine Aketch. You can call me Gera."

Loiser smiled and looked her up and down curiously. "Is my father in?"

"Yes. He is having a nap right now."

Loiser's face contorted with concern. "Why? He does not like sleeping in the afternoon. Is he sick?"

"No. He was injured on the shoulder, but he is doing well now. It's nothing serious."

Loiser quickly dashed to her father's room after tossing her her backpack on the seat.

On entering the room, she found him sound asleep. She walked stealthily and sat on the bedside chair.

***

Brandon was turning so that he could lie on his good shoulder, and opening his eyes, saw his daughter at the bedside, forlorn.

"Hi, Baby Girl," he called, smiling at her. "Come give Daddy a hug."

Loiser smiled and went to give him a warm hug, careful not to graze his injury.

"What happened to your shoulder?" she asked, reaching to lightly touch the bandage.

"I fell down."

"But grown ups don't fall down like us small children," she protested.

"That's not really true. We also fall down, but less than the small children like you," he said, tapping her nose with his middle finger. She smiled.

"Does it hurt?"

"A little, but by tomorrow, I will be fine."

"You promise?"

"I promise."

"Who is that lady in the living room?"

"Who?" he asked, still not believing that she hadn't left. "Ooh, that's Gera."

"Is she your girlfriend?"

"What do you know about girlfriends?" he asked, grinning.

"Don't answer a question with a question," she said stubbornly.

"That's my line, you little thief."

"You are my role model, Dad," she said, putting up a serious face, and they both laughed.

"Yes, she is my girlfriend."

"When are you getting married?"

"She is not my girlfriend as in lover. She is just my friend who happens to be a girl."

"You have lost me there," she said, her shoulders slumping in despair.

"When you grow up, you will understand," he convinced her.

"Can I also have a boyfriend?" she asked, her face lighting up. He looked at her disapprovingly, and she smiled before adding, "As in a friend who is a boy."

He roared with laughter, shaking his head in disbelief.

"Yes, you can, but you have to bring him home to me first, alright?"

"I'll try," she said, disappointed, but the mock glare he sent her told her that he was serious.

"Baby Girl, you need to bathe and then do your assignments."

"Okay. See you later," she said, leaving the room.

***

Gera could not help but eavesdrop on their conversation. She was again reminded of how lacking her childhood had been. She could barely recall her father's face. Thirteen years was a long time to keep the memory alive. Plus her father had always worked in Nairobi while they stayed in Oyugis. He rarely visited, and when he did, it was only for one week during which he had a flurry of activities lined up.

She hadn't taken a photo of him with her to the orphanage. On some days, she thought she had a vivid picture of her father ingrained in her mind. On other days, she had to struggle to bring his image into focus. And nowadays, his figure was blurred. Like he was standing in the doorway and light poured from behind him, causing him to become more of a silhouette.

"You are still here?" Brandon said, startling her from her daydream.

She sat up straight like a rod before turning to him at the door. He was leaning on the doorpost looking at her intently, and she felt herself warming up.

"I wanted to inform you of my departure, but you were still sleeping," she said, glad she was able to talk at all.

"But you could have woken me up. It's not right for a young lady to walk in the dark," he said, walking into the room.

It was then that Gera noted that he was only in his vest, all the muscles in his arms bulging. *This man is eye candy*, she thought, enjoying the view while it lasted.

"I did not know that it would get this late," she said, looking out and realizing it was very dark outside. It had even started to drizzle.

She didn't know how she was going to get shelter this late in the night. The only option was to go back to the orphanage, and she didn't want to bother them. She had been lucky that they had kept her with them for thirteen years. It was only logical to leave the space for the young boys and girls abandoned or orphaned.

"I can see you are better now, so I will take my leave," she said, rising up.

All of a sudden, she felt very tired. It had been stupid of her to leave Rongo the way she had. But she had been so angry that she hadn't been thinking properly. She sighed, knowing that nonetheless, she had made the right move. She could not imagine being in the same room with her mother. Who did she think she was, crawling back into their lives and expecting everything to move on as usual? It was like they could pick up from where they'd left. This time, her mother wasn't going to succeed.

The loud rumbling of her stomach filled the room. She quickly reached out to hold her tummy in a bid to quieten it down. One look at his raised eyebrow, and she felt like disappearing through some *abracadabra* magic.

"When last did you have a proper meal?"

"It is none of your business," she said, walking to the door.

"It is. First, I find you on top of my tree stealing my mangoes, then you knock me down while escaping a chameleon, and now, your stomach is roaring like you have a den of lions in there," he said, motioning to her midsection.

"Yesterday at lunch," she volunteered. There was no use fighting mouth battles with this man.

"What! Then it's only a matter of time before you drop dead in my house."

"It's not that bad. Stop exaggerating," she said, but the second rumbling made him get up to then lead her to the kitchen by the elbow.

He quickly handed her a plate of rice and beef after heating it up in the microwave. She wanted to protest that she had to leave, but the aroma and the sight of the food had her mouth watering. The stern look he gave her from across the table dried the words in her throat.

She picked up her spoon and started eating. The food was so delicious that she closed her eyes.

***

Brandon could not help but look at this woman. She had him fascinated and intrigued at the same time. These days, he found women dull and boring. He could not tell one from the other. Yet, this woman was different. She wasn't just a face in the crowd—she was *the* face. Like right now, she was devouring the food, and within five minutes, her plate was empty. She wasn't like those girls who nibbled at their food to impress the man. If at all, this woman seemed to want to get on his nerves every time.

"I have to leave now," she announced, getting up.

"I wish I could drop you in my car, but my shoulder is hurting. I doubt I can drive."

"It's okay. I will find my way."

"Are you kidding me? Let me put on a shirt and take you to the stage."

"I couldn't impose."

"I insist," he said, going out of the kitchen.

He left her staring blankly out the window. After five minutes, he came back in a T-shirt and sweater and an umbrella in the left hand. They walked to the door, and when he opened it, cold air rushed into the house. It was raining hard, and lightning covered the sky before a clap of thunder caused her to almost cling to his hand.

After the thunder had passed, he opened the umbrella, and they started walking towards the gate. Gera rubbed her hands up and down her arms. Her teeth also clattered soundly. Brandon looked down at her worriedly, but she tried to suppress the shivering. He removed his sweater and handed it to her. At first, she hesitated, eyeing him, but she finally took the garment gladly, put it on, and mumbled her gratitude.

It was very dark, and the falling rain wasn't helping matters, the road filled with puddles of water which Gera only saw after getting into. She cursed as she got out of one puddle after the other, and in spite of himself, Brandon found himself smiling.

At last, he decided to hold her hand 'til they got the stage. Her soft hand felt freezing cold in his warm one, and he rubbed his thumb over the back of her hand. When they got to the stage, she quickly withdrew it from his.

There was no *matatu* in sight. They stood in the *bodaboda* shed for twenty minutes without success.

"It's nine-forty-five p.m. There are no vehicles going to town unless you take a motorbike, but as you can see, there is none here," he said, looking at his phone, the screen light illuminating the dark space.

"I will walk."

"In this rain and darkness? No way!"

"You are not my father. You can't tell me what to do."

"True. But God help me if I have to carry you on my back, if you prove problematic."

Gera shook her head in protest. "So what are my options?"

"We go back, you sleep, and start out tomorrow."

"And risk your wife burning me with hot water! No, thanks," she said defiantly.

"I don't have a wife," he replied tersely.

"Oh. Sorry. May God rest her soul in peace."

"She is not dead, so save your prayers."

"Then where is she?"

"None of your business."

"Ooh. I see," she said, and he felt her eyes boring at him.

He unclenched his jaw and thrust his hands into his pockets.

"Let's go," he snapped.

She walked to his side, and they started back to his house.

***

Gera didn't know whether she was making the right choice, but she was out of options. She kept wondering what had happened to his wife. Not that she was complaining, anyway. She felt giddy with joy. This handsome man was single, after all.

When they arrived at his home, the warmth of the house enveloped her. Her feet were so freezing cold that they felt numb. Loiser was still at the table doing her homework, and she looked at them curiously.

"Loiser, we are hosting Gera for the night," Brandon announced.

"Alright. Welcome, Gera," Loiser said, smiling.

He led her to one of the spare bedrooms upstairs. The room was spacious and had big windows, a medium-size bed occupying the left wall. There was also a walk-in wardrobe just next to the door, as well as a small bathroom with an instant shower.

"You can use this nightie and this pyjamas and T-shirt," he said, motioning to a lacy, red nightdress, grey pants, and white T-shirt in the wardrobe.

"Thank you."

He turned and walked out without a backward glance. Gera remained standing in the middle of the room, confused. She shook her head as she went to close the door, then turned on the switch of the instant shower.

She stripped off her dirty and worn out clothes and quickly washed them before stepping under the sprinkling water, which was so warm on her body that a moan escaped her lips. It washed away the dirt and fatigue. When she finished, she felt so fresh and rejuvenated as she toweled her body with the white towel hanging on the rack.

She wrapped it around her and walked back into the room. The towel almost fell when she collided with Brandon and he held her up to steady her.

"Sorry. I wanted to give you this," he said, handing her a body lotion.

She sighed before taking it. "Is that why you almost knocked me down?"

"Sorry," he repeated, not meeting her gaze. He quickly turned to leave, cursing under his breath.

Gera smeared the chocolate-scented lotion on her body and liked how silky it felt. She then slipped on the nightie and quickly moved to the mirror. She looked so sexy and uptown. She had never looked and felt this good about herself.

She plopped on the bed, and the thick mattress absorbed her weight. This was how life was supposed to be. The orphanage beds had been so thin that the metal had poked her ribs. Most of the children also wetted their beds, making the dormitory reek of urine.

This room, however, smelt of the expensive detergents which had been used on the sheets. She covered herself with the soft blanket and tried to stay awake to enjoy its softness, but she was too tired to be aware for long, and her eyes closed.

Chapter Three

Gera woke with a start, sweating and shivering. She sat up in bed, hugging her knees. It took her a while to register her surroundings. She had dreamt of her mother. But it had been more of a flashback. She couldn't shake the sadness from the day her mother had left them in Mama Ngina Children's Orphanage.

It had been the day after her father had been buried. Her uncles had chased them away, raining insults on them. They had only been allowed time to pick up their clothes. She had been confused, could not understand why her uncles were being so mean. That evening, they'd slept in Kosele, at their family friend's house.

The next day after breakfast, her mother had left and come back at midday with a short, charcoal-black, fat man Gera had never seen. Her mother had quickly explained that he was Jarongo and he was ready to help. They'd left in the afternoon and had driven to Kisumu in his car. Gera had thought that was where the man lived, but she had been wrong. The car had halted cat Mama Ngina Children's Orphanage.

"Mama, what are we doing here?" she had asked, scared, as a dozen children rounded the car, touching it in awe.

"Listen to me, Gera. You and Queen will put up here for the night. I will come back for you tomorrow first thing in the morning."

"No, Mama, I want to go with you. Don't leave us here. I'm scared," she'd said, clinging to her mother's dress, pleading.

"I promise. You are only staying here for the night."

Gera had shaken her head in protest as tears had filled her eyes. Queen, on the other hand, had run along and was playing with the other children on the swings.

"Take care of your sister. See you tomorrow," her mother had said, hugging her tightly. She had then kissed her on the forehead and climbed into the car.

Gera had stood there watching the car leave and had broken into a wail. Queen had appeared at her side, suckling her thumb, and she, too, had started crying. The other children had looked at them, pity in their eyes.

Mama Jane, who was in charge, had come to comfort them and had told them everything was going to be alright. Her hug had been so warm, Gera had felt something akin to comfort. That night, they had slept in the dormitory which housed twenty children. The mattress had been so thin that she had kept turning the whole night because the bed's metallic rail had offered no comfort. The smell of urine had also been unbearable.

She had woken at four a.m., bathed, and put on her floral dress. She'd also woken up Queen, who'd grumbled as she bathed her. By seven o'clock, she had carried their clothes and had been sitting by the gate waiting for their mother. She'd refused to eat anything, had sat by the gate 'til night. Her mother had been nowhere to be seen.

She did this for the next one month, waiting, expecting. Her mother had never come. Years had rolled by until she had given up hope. Her resentment for her mother increased to the point of numbness.

Mama Jane had been there for her, always talking to her, encouraging her and hugging her. With time, she no longer felt lonely. She later came to learn that given enough time, you can get used to anything. Then she had fallen in love with Clinton who was also in the orphanage.

At the memory of Clinton, she felt warm and cozy. Her hands flew to her lips, and she touched them, remembering how he had always kissed her tenderly. He had promised to marry her one day and give her all her heart's desires.

She had felt herself walking on air after that. Clinton had been so true and real. She had believed that love was possible. Then, he had left, and things had changed for the worse. Although he visited once in a while, it wasn't the same. She missed their strolls in the evening when they held hands. At night, they would look up at the sky and try to name the constellations. He would then escort her to her dormitory and kiss her before whispering how much he loved her. Gera had believed that a better life was possible. But after his departure, she hadn't been so sure.

Over the years, he came less and less to the orphanage. It became clear that they were from different planets. She would bet it was because Clinton now interacted with 'normal' children, and he had no use for abandoned ones. Most of the kids in the orphanage had small dreams; she didn't know why that was so. While the 'normal' children dreamt of being lawyers, pilots, engineers, and doctors, they dreamt of being cleaners, bodaboda riders, and cooks. It had always saddened her heart that the children had lost hope in life. She later learnt that, maybe they feared failure, and that's why they had easily achievable dreams.

***

Gera sat up in bed 'til three a.m. She could not just go back to sleep and decided to wake up and get busy. She mopped the whole house, dusting and wiping the surfaces. When she had finished, she went to the laundry room where she found a small heap of clothes. She quickly washed them and hung them up to dry. She then proceeded to the kitchen where she took milk from the fridge and prepared tea.

When Loiser came downstairs to prepare tea, she found it ready.

"Good morning, Gera."

"Good morning. How was your night?"

"My night was fantastic. But it seems you didn't sleep a wink."

"How do you know?"

"Because I heard you scrubbing the floors at ungodly hours, and the house is super clean."

"I hope I didn't wake you."

"Not at all. Thanks for making my tea," Loiser said, sitting down at the table and sipping from her mug. "Please join me."

Gera sat down and poured her tea into a tall white cup.

"Which class are you in?" she asked.

"Class six."

"School must be fun, huh?"

"Sometimes, but I hate waking up early and doing assignments," Loiser said, wrinkling her nose.

Gera smiled and shook her head.

"I'm already running late. I hope to meet you when I get back from school," Loiser said, and before Gera could answer, she hugged her and rushed out of the door.

Gera loved her already. She was such a sweet little girl. What could make a woman leave such a handsome man and a pretty girl? She was still raking her brain when she heard Brandon clearing his throat as he walked into the room.

She rose up with a start. "Good morning."

"Good morning. Did you clean the house?"

"Yes. Do you have a problem with that?"

"Not really. You should have been sleeping. You are my guest."

"I could not get any sleep."

"Why is that?"

"None of your business," she said, smiling.

He took his seat as his gaze swept through his house. "Thank you. It has been a long time since my house was this clean."

"You're welcome. Here is your tea."

She handed him his mug, and their fingers brushed, lingering for a moment. His eyes flew to hers, and Gera could not look away even if she wanted to. She could not believe that the simple act was making all the blood drain from her head. What was it about this man that had all her senses on alert?

He chuckled, and she quickly withdrew her hand.

"How is your arm?" she asked, turning quickly to rinse a cup in the sink.

"It's better than yesterday. But it needs to be washed, and the bandage changed."

"I can do that for you," she said without hesitating. She turned to look at him, only to find his eyebrows raised quizzically. "What?"

"Are you always this nice early in the morning? First, you clean the house, wash my clothes, prepare my tea, and now, you are offering to change my bandage."

"Are you complaining?"

"No, but yesterday, you gave me a different side to you. I can't keep up. Which one is your real side?"

"You will find out soon enough."

"I can't wait. Let me take a shower before we can see to my arm," he said, taking his cup to the sink. He took the sponge, washed it, and put it on the rack.

Gera was impressed. This was a man who knew how to take care of himself. Not like those who waited around for the woman to do everything as if the woman were a donkey.

She listened as the shower ran and imagined him under the sprinkling water. She quickly shook her head to clear it of such intimate thoughts.

Ten minutes later, he breezed into the room as his scent filled the air; it was a mixture of his soap, his aftershave, and cologne. *A heady combination.* He was clad in a pair of brown khaki shorts exposing hairy toned legs and a form-fitting green T-shirt.

"I'm ready," he said, leading the way to his bedroom, and she followed like a bull being led to the slaughter.

He had great legs, she noted and swallowed.

Brandon removed his shirt and lay on the bed. Gera looked around his room and saw that his bed was well spread and everything in order. This man was something, she thought and smiled.

The warm water and disinfectant had been laid near the bed. She removed yesterday's bandage carefully, and he winced in pain. The wound was covered with a scab, which was a good sign. She dipped the piece of cloth in water and wiped around the wound to clean traces of blood. She also massaged the area around to ease the tension. When she had finished, he sighed, flexing his arm.

"Thank you very much," he said, putting on his shirt.

"You are welcome. I should be on my way now."

"Let me drive you."

"Are you sure you can drive?"

"Positive."

"Let's go, then," she said.

***

"This is it," she said when they arrived at Mama Ngina Children's Orphanage in Kibuye.

"What are we doing here? As far as I can tell, you are not a child," Brandon enquired, staring at her bosom, and she felt herself shiver with something akin to excitement. He winked at her as he unfastened his safety belt.

Gera opened her door and jumped to the ground.

"Goodbye, Brandon. It was nice meeting you," she said, extending her hand.

He looked at it and didn't take it. Instead, he pulled her into a warm hug that left her breathless. She walked away, leaving him looking after her.

The boys surrounded the car, touching it. It reminded her of her first day in the orphanage. It was funny how she had wanted to leave on that first day, yet today, she had come of her own free will. Whether she liked it or not, this was her home. She had read of a poet who was trying to define a home. Is home where your clothes are? Is home a built structure? Is home comprised of people who really care about each other? In the end, the poet had concluded that home is where your heart is.

Mama Jane was waiting on the veranda, arms wide open. Gera walked into them and let her embrace her. There was something comforting about Mama Jane's hugs—they were warm, caring, and motherly.

"Are you alright?" Mama Jane asked, caressing her cheeks.

"I'm fine."

"I missed you. Let's go and take tea," she said as they went to her office.

They drank sweet tea with *maandazis*.

"So, who is he?"

"Who?" Gera feigned innocence.

"That man in a Mercedes-Benz."

"Some Good Samaritan."

"I don't believe you. I saw you, remember. He was looking at you like ..."

"Like what?"

"He was really into you, but I wasn't sure. Then he pulled you into a hug, and I confirmed it. You like him, don't you?"

"No," she lied, and Mama Jane poked her in the ribs. "Ouch! I was in love with Clinton, but when he was adopted by that rich family, things changed."

"That was Clinton. Both of you were still too young to know what love means."

"I don't know why, but everyone I love usually disappears from my life."

"That's not entirely true. I am here for you always, don't forget that. What happened to you and your mother?"

"It's a long story. I can't believe it took me a whole two weeks to realize that I could not live with her. Whenever I look at her, I feel my anger rising. No apologies, no remorse. She thinks that just because we are her children, we should forgive her," she said, throwing her hands in the air. "Today, I could not take it anymore. She started shouting at me, telling me that I was ungrateful and selfish. Telling me to grow up and stop behaving like a brat. I am an adult and can fend for myself, I no longer need her anyway, so I left. Queen chose to stay back. I didn't have anywhere else to go," she said, tears welling up her eyes.

"You know you are always welcome here," Mama Jane told her, rubbing her back.

She roughly wiped the tears away with the back of her right hand, though she could not shake away the cold and dread that crept up her spine whenever she thought that she was not enough, not deserving of love. Mama Jane had once told her, "Gera, the pain of not being loved, especially when it happens at a time that you need it the most, is unbearable."

Was that to remain her fate?

***

When Brandon got back home, he felt some kind of emptiness, like he were missing a vital part of his being. His feet led him to the room Gera had slept the night in. He didn't know whether it was to recapture her image in the room or to see if she had left anything he could keep as a souvenir.

He sat on the well-made bed trying to imagine her lying on the mattress, walking around the room, using the shower. That reminded him of how he had walked in when he'd heard her moan under the water. It had awakened a sleeping giant in him. He had stepped to the door to listen in for another moan when she had walked out of the bathroom, almost knocking him down.

Then he remembered their fingers brushing earlier that morning. He had felt irresistible forces flow through him at that single accidental touch. The last memory was when he had openly ogled at her boobs when he'd told her that she was too old to be in the orphanage. He'd seen the way she had shivered, and he was convinced he wasn't in this alone.

He saw a glittering object near the wardrobe and went to pick it. It was a metallic bangle. He had seen her wearing a dozen of them.

He had to take this to her. It was trivial, and he knew he should dismiss it, but he couldn't. He was planning to take it to her in the evening after picking Loiser from school. The mere thought that he was going to see her again sent his heart beating fast.

He kept looking at his watch as he did some work on his laptop. When four p.m. finally arrived, he drove to town. It took him ten minutes to get to the school. Loiser jumped onto the seat next to him.

"Good evening Dad. Your arm has healed?"

"Yes. I told you it would heal today, didn't I?"

"That's awesome. Is Gera still at home?"

"I'm afraid she left," he said, and saw how her face lost its smile.

She didn't talk much 'til they got home. He didn't even try to break the silence, too preoccupied with his thoughts.

"Take your bath and then start on your assignment. I will be back by six p.m.," he said when they arrived home. Loiser got out of the car and walked slowly to the front door.

He sped to the orphanage to bridge the gap between him and Gera. When he arrived there, some children were still swinging on the swings. He got out of his car and walked to the office, the evening breeze fanning his face and the smell of simmering ugali meeting his nose.

"Welcome, sir. Have a seat," the older woman said, extending her hand in greeting.

He read the plaque on the dark brown wooden table, inscribed with 'Mama Jane Otieno.' His gaze swept the room which had paint crawling away form the wall, the ceiling with brown patches.

"Thank you, madam."

"Please call me Mama Jane. How can I help you?"

"I have come to see Gera," he said, shifting in his seat when he saw how her eyes were trained on him.

"And who are you?"

"I'm Brandon Odhiambo."

"She is at the swings. You didn't see her on your way in?"

"No, I didn't."

"Just give me a minute," she said, rising from her seat.

He followed her out. From the pavement, he saw her seated on the swing with about half a dozen children. One was on her lap holding onto her tightly as the swing went high up. Their laughter filled the air as those swinging pushed it even higher so that they plucked leaves from a nearby tree.

Something about her expression pulled him to look at it. Her face was lit up, and the fading rays of the sun played on it, making her look surreal, like she was illuminated from inside out. Her eyes were also bright as she laughed out loud.

He stood transfixed to the spot. Never in his life had he seen something this beautiful or even imagined that such beauty existed. He couldn't look away. Something stirred in him, and almost immediately, he knew what he had to do. He had never been so sure about anything in his life. There was just something about this woman that he knew was rare. He doubted if he was ever going to find another like her that could make his blood boil in his veins.

Gera shifted her eyes from the sky, and she and the child landed on the pavement. Time stood still as she looked into his eyes.

***

What was he doing here? she wondered as she told the children to stop the swing. She got off, put on her sandals, and began walking towards him, their eyes never leaving each other.

"What are you doing here?" she asked, and the disapproval on Mama Jane's face made her change tact. "Sorry. Good evening."

"Good evening," Brandon said, smiling mockingly.

"You can use my office," Mama Jane announced, going to the kitchen.

They went there, and Gera sat on Mama Jane's seat as Brandon took the visitor's seat. She was comforted by the professional distance the table in between them created.

"I brought you this," he said, handing her the bangle.

She took it and added it to the ones already on her wrist. "Thank you. Are you sure that such a small item had you driving all the way from Mamboleo?"

"Yes. What other reason would I have for coming back here?" he asked, chuckling to himself.

"I don't know. You tell me."

"I have a business proposal for you."

"I'm listening."

"I want you to come help me with the household chores," he said, crossing his right ankle over his left knee.

"Excuse me?"

"Yes, you heard me. You will clean the floors, cook, and do laundry."

"Ooh," was all she managed.

She was desperate to leave the orphanage and make something of her life. Being a maid was low class, but she had to start from somewhere, right? And besides, she didn't even have a college education to brag about.

"Let's say I happen to accept this job. How much are you going to pay me?"

"Ten thousand shillings."

"Make it fifteen."

"Fine."

She looked at him for a while, registering the impact of all this.

"Are you sure about this?" she asked timidly. She just hoped this wasn't a dream she was going to wake up from.

"I'm as serious as I will ever be," he said, uncrossing his legs.

"Let me inform Mama Jane, then." She grinned, rushing out of the room.

She was gone for a while and came back with Mama Jane in tow.

"Take care of my girl," she told Brandon, and they left.

Mama Jane stood at the pavement, waving as they drove out of the gate.

Chapter Four

It was Saturday, and for the first time in years, Brandon was happy that he wasn't going to the office. Usually, he would have stayed in bed, but not on his day. His thoughts were not at rest. He could have pretended to have no idea why, but deep inside, he knew it was Gera who was haunting his dreams.

He got out of bed and went into the kitchen to prepare tea. He wanted to watch the sunrise. It was a magnificent sight which he didn't fail to admire whenever he felt in the mood. His bedroom window faced east, and when Jackie was here, they used to enjoy the sight together.

But after she'd left, for a while, he didn't like the habit because it only brought up memories that were better left where they were. Some people took sunrise for granted, but not Brandon. He saw it as that little piece of magic that came out every morning even when times were hard to remind them that everyday held a potential for beauty.

He went to his room with the jug of tea and sat on the chair by the window as he waited for the sun. Thoughts of Gera got the better part of his mind and heart. Since the very first time he had set eyes on her, he had known that he'd found what he was looking for. He felt like she was the woman meant for him.

He hadn't thought of anyone like that, not even Jackie, and the realization shocked him. And he wondered, just for once, whether the deceptive leaving of Jackie was a blessing in disguise, after all.

He was so deep in his thoughts that when he heard shuffling and footsteps, he sat up straight, then stood up and went to the window. Parting the curtains, he saw Gera in the field. She wore a pair of black slacks and a white T-shirt.

What the heck was that woman doing in the field? From his observation, she was jogging. Things were just getting better and better. From the window, he had a clear view, and instead of cursing, he decided to enjoy it. Her body movements were driving him crazy, and for a moment, he thought Gera was torturing him deliberately. That pair of breasts was going to be his undoing.

***

When Gera saw Brandon's bedroom door slightly opened, she couldn't resist the temptation to peep in just to see what he was up to. He was in deep thoughts, and she wondered just what he was thinking about. Was it his work or his wife? She did not want to interrupt him and thus just proceeded to the kitchen.

She had decided from the day she got out of her mother's home that she wasn't going to be sad. She had been sad enough, always playing by the tunes made by others. Enough was enough. She wanted to play her own tunes. It was time to look out for her happiness first, even though it sounded selfish. All she wanted was to have fun and happiness. Life was too short, and one should enjoy every moment, she thought with a smile.

She prepared tea, set it on table, and went outside. It was chilly out, but she was not going to give up.

The first thing she wanted was to be in good shape, and she had decided to do some laps outside the house. The field was very big, and she knew that when she finished one lap, she would be very tired. She fastened her braids with a rubber band, then warmed up before she started jogging. She jogged a bit, and already, her muscles were paining. She almost gave up, but this was something she had promised herself to do.

She had forgotten about Brandon, but she got a feeling while jogging that she was being watched. The only suspect that came to mind was him. She looked up at his window, caught him grinning sheepishly.

She held her ground and continued jogging although when she finished one lap, she was sweating, panting, and tired.

When she returned to the house, she met Brandon on the way. She greeted him and rushed to her room, where she showered and changed into clean clothes. Today, she felt like flirting, so she put on a pair of black shorts and a pink T-shirt inscribed with '*You are a naughty boy go to my room*' then marched out. She felt so alive and her heart free. She wanted to do things, talk, smile, and just be happy.

When she came out, she found both Loiser and Brandon at the table waiting for her, and she felt guilty for making them wait. Loiser gave her a peck as she smiled at her dad knowingly.

Everyone served tea, and within minutes, they were chatting freely.

"Gera, please tell us about your home?" Loiser pleaded with her.

Who could refuse such a request, when it came from such a sweet girl? Gera already had such a soft spot for her.

"It's a good village. It is called Koyucho. People are kind, they care for each other. We collected firewood from the hills; we went to the river to fetch water and also swim. It's such a good place, so peaceful and full of love," she said nostalgically.

For a moment, she was back there, being happy, being free, but that had been before her father's death. Her happy times and memories had been tarnished by sadness, betrayal, and so much hatred.

She eyed Brandon and saw his eyebrows knit in concern. Tears pooled in her eyes, and she saw goosebumps form on her arms. She resisted the urge to cry, and rubbed her hands up and down her arms instead.

Loiser got off her seat and held her so tightly that she felt like being herself and weeping her heart out. She had wept for so long that she didn't think she had any more tears left. Brandon, too, stood up and came to comfort her, softly squeezing her arms. He felt her pain, as well, but maybe in his own way. They both hugged her so warmly, so tenderly, that Gera felt more tears forming in her eyes.

From that moment onwards, it was like there was a special kind of bond among the three of them. Being far away from home maybe was going to give her the peace of mind and clarity she needed, she concluded.

***

Loiser arrived home from school at five o'clock. She rushed ahead into the house while Brandon trailed behind her.

"Wow! Gera, what are you cooking? It smells so good," she announced, barging into the kitchen after dropping her school bag on the seat.

"Someone is back from school," Gera said, turning to her.

"Yes, and very hungry," Loiser replied, stirring the food boiling in the sufuria. "What is this?"

"Egg curry."

"How is it prepared?"

"First, you boil the eggs for about fifteen minutes, then dip them in cold water for them to cool down. After that, you peel them," she explained, and Loiser nodded, taking in all the details.

"Why do we use all these *dhania, pilipili hoho, tangawizi, and kitungu saumu?*" Loiser asked curiously.

"My mother used to call it cooking with love. This is whereby you mix all the natural ingredients to produce a delicious meal."

"Can I have a taste?"

"Of course," Gera said, handing her a table spoon.

She blew on the soup before sipping it. "It tastes even better. You know, my mother didn't like cooking. And when she did, it was so bitter that I would always add sugar."

"How did it taste after adding sugar?" Gera asked, laughing.

"It would taste even worse," Loiser admitted. "I miss her."

"Where did she go?" she asked, fearing where this conversation was leading to.

Loiser sat on the chair so slowly, as if the question had weakened her knees. Gera turned off the gas cooker and sat by the table.

"She left with Dad's friend, Ken," she said simply, then kept quiet.

Gera was afraid to ask any more questions.

Then the girl started talking again, her eyes gaining a far away look. "I came home from school one day and found her in the living room together with my father and Ken. She had all her bags packed. I didn't know what to do, so I hid behind the door and listened in. My father had always told me that it was bad manners to listen in on adults' conversation, but I had to this time."

"Disobedient girl," Gera teased to lighten the air which was so thick.

"They were all arguing and shouting. At some point, it got too much, and I covered my ears. I was so afraid. My mother was saying that she was leaving with Ken for good. My father begged her to stay, if not for him then for me. I knew then that I had to do something. I walked in on them, and they were surprised and stopped arguing for a while. I begged my mother to stay. I even promised never to wet my bed if she stayed. Do you know what she did?"

Gera shook her head.

"She just dragged her suitcases out and went with that man. I followed them, wailing and pleading. But she didn't even look back. She got into the car, and they drove away. I sat on the doorsteps looking into thin air, confused. My father joined me. I looked into his eyes and saw them red with unshed tears. 'What are we going to do?' I asked. He gave me a weak smile and said, 'We will survive.' He held me as I cried. That night, we slept hungry. No one was in the mood to eat. But you know what happened the next day?"

Gera shook her head again.

"The sun rose, the clock worked fine, vehicles were moving as usual. The world was fine. I was mad at everyone and everything. I refused to go to church. If God loved us, then He shouldn't have allowed this to happen to us. My father started drinking heavily. I guess he was trying to survive. I would cry myself every night to sleep. Our lives were pathetic.

"Then I don't know how it happened, but my father stopped drinking. We had a lengthy talk, and he told me that we could not go on like this. We started going out every weekend. He would help me with my homework. He would cook meals instead of eating out all the time. And life wasn't so bad, after all. Then, my mother came to see me in school ..."

"What happened?" Gera asked, holding her hand.

"I was happy to see her at first. She is my mother, you know. I wanted to even run to her and embrace her, but then I remembered everything. I felt my heart bursting with so much hatred for her. I ran away."

"Sorry," was all Gera managed to say as she hugged her.

They hugged for a while, before Loiser pulled away, wiping her tears with her sweater.

***

When Gera served dinner that night, it was a quiet affair. After what Loiser had told her, she had more questions than answers in her head. Why was life sometimes so unfair? Did Loiser's mother ever find what she looking for in Ken? How did Brandon feel now that the worst had passed?

She looked up at him. He was eating his meal, oblivious of her stare. This man was perfect. He was tall, dark, and handsome. He had money. He was quite the gentleman. Jackie didn't know how much she had lost, and Gera doubted if she was ever going to find such a man again.

She cleared the table and washed the utensils before retiring for the night, though she stayed up for most of it. Warm tears inched down her cheeks to wet her pillow. She cried for Loiser, for Brandon, for Queen and herself.

When she stopped crying, she felt so much relieved, and then, she slept.

Chapter Five

Brandon came home from work only to find Gera in the field playing with Loiser and her friends from school. He had to pinch himself to be sure that he wasn't dreaming. She threw the ball and ran around the field, her skirt knotted at the side, exposing her fleshy thighs.

When Gera and Loiser entered the house, they were surprised to find him in the sitting room. They had been too engaged in their game to even notice that he was already home. The disapproving look he gave them must have made them feel like two little girls who were being reprimanded.

When he burst out with laughter, they joined him, not knowing what the laughter was all about. But it didn't really matter. Gera was dirty; she had dirt all over her clothes and small patches of dust all over her face. The same applied to Loiser. But it was Gera's case that made him laugh more. For Loiser, it was acceptable, but for Gera—what had the woman been thinking? She was twenty-one years old, for God's sake, he thought, shaking his head.

Gera and Loiser looked at each other conspiratorily and went to him with open arms, ready to hug him. He tried to escape but it was too late; he was already cornered. Wicked girls, he thought. They hugged him, smearing him with dirt all over.

Brandon loved the hugs from Gera. If dirt was the price he had to pay to receive such closeness, he was more than willing. He felt her tender breasts rest on his chest, and he allowed his imagination to travel further. What if they didn't have the clothes on? Skin on skin. How would it feel?

He swallowed and searched her eyes. Their gazes held for some time before she ran off to her room to clean up. He and Loiser each went to their respective rooms because everyone now needed a bath.

When Loiser and Gera came down to prepare supper, they found him at it.

"Hi, ladies," he greeted them, and they chorused a reply.

"Do you need help?" Gera asked him.

"No, just sit down. You two can tell me stories while I cook," he replied.

Gera and Loiser sat down at the table exchanging mischievious glances which he didn't understand. Gera was a breath of fresh air in their lives. He realized that since she had come, he was happier than he'd ever been in his life. He was always in a rush to get home these days. He was jovial and more productive at his job. Sometimes, he would watch as she patiently explained to Loiser the recipes of different meals.

For a moment, he would imagine that this was his family—Gera was his wife, and he was always coming home to her. The image was so perfect and vivid. He was almost sure that if he extended his hands, he could touch it.

Loiser, too, was performing better at her class work and the midterm exams. She was now among the best pupils in her class, and she complained that it made some students very jealous of her.

He heard some whispers and giggling from them. When he turned to face them, they put up serious faces, and he wondered just what they had up their sleeves this time. The two helped in setting the table when he was through with cooking. They ate supper in a jovial mood.

He watched as Gera ate the food slowly, savouring the taste.

"How do you find the food, girls?" he asked after sometime.

"Excellent!" they chorused.

When they had finished eating, the bowls were empty, a clear indication that they had loved the food. He was happy for that. It was a long time since he'd cooked.

Loiser announced that she had assignments to finish and then disappeared to her room. He and Gera were left in the kitchen alone. Loiser seemed to have gone with the merry mood, and now, awkward silence hung thick in the air.

***

Brandon glanced up at Gera and winked. She quickly looked down at the table, drawing patterns with her right index finger.

"I can do with a little help in washing up. I don't fancy it that much," he announced, carrying the plates to the sink, and she followed him with the bowls.

They washed the utensils in silence, one in which she felt uncomfortable, and she started humming some tuneless song.

He was the one rinsing the plates, and he poured water on her feet deliberately. She stopped her humming and eyed him dangerously.

"Sorry for that, miss," he apologized in a soft tone she almost believed until she saw the smug look on his face.

She decided not to give him the satisfaction of getting angry and went on with her washing.

Brandon again poured water on her feet. She did not react.

The third time he did that, he got what he was looking for. She poured a cupful of soapy water on his face. The water stung his eyes, and he quickly reached out to get clean water which he used to wash away the soap.

He eyed her, anger burning through his gaze. She looked at him daringly, goading him to try another move. Truth be told, she was very scared of the cold look she received from him. What was he going to do her? But he was the one who had started it—she'd just defended herself.

"What now? Bring it on. I am shaking in my boots!" she dared him, knowing she was biting more than she could swallow.

"Young lady, are you daring me, by any chance?" he asked, his gaze intent on her, and she knew she was in deep trouble.

"Take it however you want. Come on, Lover Boy," she continued. What could he possibly do to her? *Nothing.*

He moved a step towards her, and she took a step behind.

"Why are you moving behind when you seemed so courageous some seconds ago?" he teased her.

"Because you have moved a step closer, so it is only logical to move a step behind, don't you think?"

He moved even closer, and she stepped behind until her back met the cold metallic door. She opened it and went out. Brandon followed her out.

It was dark outside, and it took some time before their eyes got accustomed to the absence of light, but not before she stumbled and fell on the ground. Brandon also did not see the log early enough, and he fell with a thud on her. She cursed, and he apologized sincerely this time. His heavy weight pressed her on the cushiony grass, but that, somehow, was the least of her problems at the moment. His hard muscles moulded onto her soft flesh.

Gera looked up and saw the full moon. She had heard stories that on the nights of the full moon, strange things happened. She wondered if she was to wait for her fate and see what it had in store for her.

"I have got you now."

He smiled at her, his warm breath fanning her face, and her heart skipped a mighty beat. But she'd be damned if she was going to show him just how affected she was by his proximity.

"What do you want?" she asked, and without intending to, her voice trembled.

She looked into his face that was now illuminated dimly by the kitchen light and the moon. His eyes were dark pools of desire caressing her face, looking deep into her eyes, straight to her soul. She watched his eyes move from her eyes to her lips, and his Adam's apple bobbed as he swallowed.

When his eyes connected with hers again, she could not keep still, and her hands fisted the dewy grass at her sides. Her tongue swiped at her lips, and his eyes, now dark as the night, followed the motion.

"I want this," he said, his voice hoarse.

When his tender, thin lips connected with her soft, thick ones, he paused, as if savoring the feel. When a moan escaped her lips straight into his, he groaned, and his tongue glided into her warm mouth.

Her eyes closed as she took him in, her hands now caressing his head, ears, and bristly jaws. When her tongue connected with his, dueling, she squirmed. He deepened the kiss, taking her mouth hostage. Warmth coursed through her body.

Just when she thought it could not get any better, he started moving, rubbing his body on hers, creating sweet friction. His hard chest scraped her boobs, and they pebbled and weighed heavy as his pace increased. His rough pair of jeans stroked her core.

"Nooo!" she cried out, though her body didn't mean it, because it wanted him so much.

"Yes, baby, feel me."

She felt his hard-on pushing forward, seeking her core, connecting with it through their clothes. She rounded her hips to meet him halfway, caressing his back through his T-shirt that was now damp with his sweat.

He suddenly stopped moving and looked into her eyes, his heart beating frantically against her, his face glistening with sweat.

"Wow! You are amazing," he said breathlessly, his lips grazing hers.

He looked at her tenderly, and they were held so tightly in the magic of the moment that neither of them could speak for a while.

"That is what I want," he announced. "For now."

He got up and helped her to her feet. They then walked arm in arm back to the house.

Indeed, on the night of the full moon, strange things do happen, she thought, smiling.

Chapter Six

Gera could not get any sleep. She kept on turning and tossing for the better part of the night. The images of the full moon kiss could not leave her mind. What would Brandon think of her now? She hadn't known that he was such a good kisser.

The thought made her long for another kiss.

Where would their relationship lead to? To a roll in the hay, or to a lifelong commitment bonded with love? Or would it end just like it did with Clinton?

She didn't want Brandon only for one night. She would be the happiest woman on Earth if she were to spend every waking morning and sunset by his side. He was everything she wanted in a man. What a life they would have! But unfortunately, that was not going to happen, because she knew that Brandon did not even love her.

Maybe their bodies were compatible, but not their hearts. Then, a thought crossed her mind. Someone once said, 'Why worry about the future you are uncertain about and yet, you have the present right here and now. Live it to the fullest and don't think about the past or the future.'

She then decided that she was going to enjoy the moment while it lasted and stop worrying about the future which wasn't even guaranteed. If things worked out well, good. But if not, at least she had memories of their moments spent together.

Her thoughts finally at rest, she drifted off to sleep.

***

Brandon, too, could not sleep. He'd known that kissing her would be good, but he had underestimated just how good it would be. Whatever there was between them was not just some simple passing fling. It was something bigger than him, something stronger that really shook him to the core. He had kissed many girls before Gera, but with her, he'd felt something unique, something special.

He remembered her asking him what he wanted just before he'd kissed her. A number of answers had crossed his mind. He wanted the kind of love that lasted forever. He wanted her to be the mother of his babies. He wanted her to be first thing he saw when he woke up in the morning.

He did not just want to have her physically; he wanted every part that constituted her—her heart, body, and soul. Could it be that he was falling in love already? But he had fallen in love once with Jackie ... yet, it had never left like this. Was that the only reason as to why he had difficulty in accepting this?

He had not intended it to be so, but his heart was just shy of loving again. He decided to give it time and see what happened. Something told him that with time, what they felt for each other would only grow stronger. He smiled and went to sleep.

He was drifting off when the grinding of metal woke him up. Curiosity got the better of him, and he went out of his room to find out. He did not like the feel of it already. The sound was coming from Gera's room. He would not forgive himself if something happened to her.

As he neared her door, he heard her scream and rushed into the room. He found her bundled in one corner of the bed, shivering, and her face was pale. He saw the curtains were drawn back, a gaping hole in the glass.

He rushed to the window to look out and saw a dark figure disappearing into the night towards the end of the field. He was tempted to give it a chase but quickly realized it was pointless. Damn! Why did this have to happen on a night the watchman was off duty? One look at Gera, and he went to her. She looked so vulnerable. He held her in his arms and comforted her until the shaking stopped. She was still very scared.

He carried her to his room and met Loiser at the door. Gera's screaming had woken her up, too. He then decided that it was best if they all stayed in his room for the night so that he was able to look out for them.

Who could the intruder be? he wondered to himself. Maybe it was a thief who wanted to steal something, but that didn't convince him much. He just felt that the person who had come there tonight had more than stealing in mind. Who hated him that much to break into his house in the middle of the night?

He only knew one enemy—Ken—but that was years ago. Furthermore, he had taken his wife, and Brandon was the aggrieved party.

Thoughts kept criss-crossing his head, but he didn't get any answer.

Loiser slept in his room, taking the bed next to his, which she usually used whenever she didn't want to go to her room. Gera was in his bed, still shaken, and he didn't want to disturb her. Maybe in the morning, she was going to be able to explain what had transpired.

He switched off the lights, and they all went to sleep. Gera's hands and legs were freezing cold because of fear. He moved closer to her and cuddled her to him to give her warmth. She fitted so well into his body.

If only this were real …

***

She had just wanted to see them, but she also knew she couldn't walk through the door. Brandon was still mad at her and didn't want anything to do with her after she had run off with his best friend, Ken. She had even gone to Loiser's school to see her, but what did she receive from that brat?

At first, Loiser had been happy to see her, and Jackie Odhiambo had even thought she was going to run to her and hug her, but her happiness had been short–lived. Loiser's face had changed to that of sadness, hurt, and then anger, and she'd run off.

She had thought the grass was greener on the other side, but she had been dead wrong. That was the worst decision she had ever made, and she knew she'd live to regret it for a lifetime. Ken was a drunkard. He didn't pay the bills, and to top it all up, he beat her every night like she was some kind of drum. She felt goosebumps when she thought of how she hated him. One day, she was going to get even with him.

She'd gone to A to Z Boutique in town to buy black boots, a black jacket, hat, and gloves for a disguise.

The need to see them was so great that she could not resist. She had gone to the place she had once called her home at around dusk and hid behind a thicket. From there, she'd had a clear view of everything that went on in the house. She saw her Brandon. He was still as handsome as she remembered. And that body—oh, my, a body many girls would kill for.

She then saw Loiser. Her sweet Loiser was growing up to be a beautiful woman. She was an adolescent now, and Jackie knew right then, Loiser needed her more than ever. Her chest hurt that she could not even be there whenever she was needed the most.

She had been deep in her thoughts when she was bolted back to reality by this woman. Who was she? Was she the new maid? That could not be. The manner in which Brandon and Loiser related with her was way more intimate than how one interacted with the maid. It was like she was the woman of the house. The lustful looks Brandon gave her ... Oh, my, and he'd never even looked at her with the same intensity in all their years of marriage.

She'd felt a huge load of jealousy descend upon her body. Loiser, too, was clinging around her as they exchanged giggles. She would have given a million shillings just to be the one with them. She'd been given the chance, but what had she done with it? Thrown it to the dogs, she thought sadly.

The girl had to be warned that she was treading on dangerous waters. Jackie decided to stay and only confront her when everyone had gone to sleep. It was freezing cold outside, but all the same, she would stay. She heard some hissing sound and only knew too well what that meant, a snake. She remained motionless, and the snake slithered away, glistening in the moonlight.

She was too petrified and was just about to give up and go when she saw the back door open and the girl get out. Fate was finally doing her a favour. She wouldn't have to wait long, after all.

When Brandon followed the girl, her heart sank. She witnessed all the kissing and the way he looked deep into the eyes of this girl. It had taken all she had not to throw a huge stone at that face, at that body which she had held in her arms so tenderly.

If the girl thought she could steal away her Brandon, then she didn't know what she was up against.

Chapter Seven

Brandon was awake at four o'clock. He was glad when the first thing he saw upon waking was Gera. Her head still rested on his chest, and she looked so divine in her sleep. He listened to her baby breaths as they formed a soft rhythm. She was such a beautiful sight, especially with the moon's illumination.

It was unfortunate that it had taken some scheming figure in the night to get her this close. He knew then that he would want to see her every day first thing in the morning.

He could have gone on lying there, but he had a lot of things to do before daybreak. He planted a soft kiss on her lips as he rolled slowly from the bed. She stirred a little but went back to sleep after a while.

He went to prepare tea, as he normally did in the mornings before he got down to business. It usually gave him a head start. In those early hours, a serene atmosphere usually prevailed over the world. He always got so much done in the morning, plus if he wanted to really excel in the competitive business world, he couldn't afford to waste those precious hours.

He had wanted to own a company, and now that the opportunity had presented itself, he couldn't resist it. In two months' time, he was going to be the manager of a company. It felt so good. Nothing could give someone as much pleasure as loving what they did and doing what they loved. It gave a person so much freedom and happiness.

Ken had thought that by stealing his wife, he had taken everything from him. Brandon had stopped going to work, and if at all he went, he was very grumpy. Then he finally stopped going altogether. All he did was drink alcohol all day and night.

The wake-up call had come when he'd realized that he had less than half a million in his bank account. A meager amount, if you took into consideration his luxurious lifestyle. He then knew that he had to get up and work. He was not going to mourn forever, especially when Jackie was still alive and kicking. They just had to survive somehow.

A piece of article he read on the Internet just went a long way to strengthen his resolve. And it went like, 'When the door of happiness is closed, another one opens, but often times, we spend so much time looking at the closed door that we don't even see the one that has been opened for us.' From then onwards, he had started looking ahead just in case another door opened. After all, there was always no chance that the closed door was going to reopen.

The Aga Khan Hospital had terminated his contract by then, and he was not in the mood to look for another job. He had then started selling drugs in his own pharmacy using his remaining money. At first, the business didn't give such promising results, but after a while, it started picking up. He was even able to open other chains around town. When the money got big, he was able to buy off other dwindling drug chemists at relatively low price then develop them to their full potential. When he was sure that the business was very stable, he decided to venture into the real estate business. He built homes in Mamboleo and later sold them at unimaginable profits.

He was back on his feet in terms of money, and he was hopeful that the rest would follow. If Ken were to strike again, Brandon knew that this time, he was more than ready for him. Ken would find a formidable opponent, and Brandon knew that nobody was going to prevent his star from shining.

He continued with his work on the iPad as he sipped his tea.

***

Gera got up at five o'clock, and it took her a while to register where she was. Brandon's bed was so comfy and she was warm, but she realized that he wasn't beside her. All night, he had held her so close and comforted her to sleep.

She got up, washed her face, brushed her teeth, and headed to his study room. Loiser was still dead asleep. The yesternight's invader had kept them up until late.

She gave the door a soft knock before entering into the study to find him buried deep in his work. She suddenly felt guilty for disrupting him. He looked up from his work and smiled at her.

"Good morning, beautiful."

"'Morning," she answered.

Did anyone have the right to be this damn handsome especially in the morning? she wondered.

"Have a seat," he told her.

"Sorry for disturbing you," she apologized after sitting down opposite him.

"Don't apologize. I was just waiting for you." He convinced her by putting away his iPad and the writing materials. "Please, Gera, tell me about last night."

"There's nothing much to say except that suddenly, someone was pounding on my window. At first, I thought it was only a dream, but on waking up, I actually saw someone at the window trying to force his way through. I was too scared to even move a muscle. I got some breath in my lungs and managed to scream for help. The next time I tried screaming, the sound was congealed in my throat and I couldn't even utter a single word. The invader heard you coming and ran into the night. Brandon, I was so scared."

Gera finished off, and the blood drained from her face again just from reliving the incident. Brandon was listening intently. He was so engaged in her narration that when she finished, it took him some time to recover.

She rubbed her hands up and down her bare arms, her eyes frantic. He rose up to his tall frame and went around the desk, taking the seat next to hers. His eyes softened as he scanned her face, and he pulled her into his lap. Warmth crept up her neck when he traced the outline of her tender, long throat with his nose, his warm breath making her squirm. She wound her hands around his neck, inching closer to him.

He pulled just an inch from her to look at her face and then smiled. She was about to confront him about what he was looking at, but he placed his index finger across her mouth, barring her from saying anything. He then traced her face with his hand, mastering her eyes, nose, mouth, ears. And everywhere he touched, he left a tingly feeling. She didn't remember being touched so tenderly and ever feeling like that whenever her face was touched.

At first, she was afraid to look up, afraid of what her eyes might show.

He raised her chin with his thumb, caressing it, and she looked up into his eyes. Their gazes held for sometime.

Gera was on her own voyage, discovering and exploring. For a moment, just a second, Brandon's guard was down, and she read something that left her wondering, worried and confused. She saw conflict in his dark brown eyes, a battle of will. He was possibly having trust issues, probably because of his ex-wife, she mused. Maybe the situation had affected him in a deeper way than he deemed possible.

She felt like helping him, reaching out to him, make him realize that he could trust her, that she would not let him down, and that she would always be there for him.

Where had those thoughts come from? Whoever said that the eyes are the windows to the soul?

Gera realized that if she did not run away now, maybe it was going to be too difficult for her to take a step later. It was not that she didn't trust Brandon. It was herself she was worried about. Since the kiss, it seemed there was just this thing that kept attracting her, pushing her towards Brandon, pulling her to him like a moth being attracted to light.

She bolted out of the room before things got out of hand. He just chuckled as he returned to his work, whistling.

Chapter Eight

Brandon and Gera recorded their statements at Mamboleo Police Station, and they were given an OB number. He now had to cross his fingers and hope the police will do their work. He had a hunch that it was not going to take long before the person came back, and he promised himself that if the intruder returned, the person was not going to be successful in leaving scot-free.

He was headed to his office when he saw Ken. He had thought that his hurting and pain had gone away, but on seeing Ken, he felt a churning in his stomach. He took a step forward, and Ken looked at him challengingly and started moving towards him.

When they got within spitting distance, Brandon was tempted to give him a punch so that when Jackie saw him, she wouldn't even recognize him. However, he was not going to give Ken the satisfaction of venting out his anger.

"Long time, no see," Ken said.

Ken was tall, but not as tall as Brandon. In the looks department, he was average-looking, a fact that annoyed him. This was because when they were in college, Brandon was given that look of 'I wish you were mine' by the girls while Ken received smiles saying 'No, thanks.' It always seemed that it was

Brandon shining in bright light, but Ken was cast in the shadow, invisible.

"Where have you been, my friend?" Brandon asked with an enthusiasm he didn't really feel. After the initial greeting, there was a slight silence during which they were sizing each other up. "What's up? You don't look as good as I expected. You have lost some pounds of flesh. Don't tell me Jackie is not treating you right," he teased him, prepared for anything.

He knew that Ken had a volatile temper, and it was soon going to erupt. Brandon was subtle in handling anger. He never lost his cool. He never let it bubble out, and he just enjoyed seeing the anger in Ken's eye.

"On the contrary, we are fine. She's happier by my side than she had been with you. Did you know that Jackie had our son not long ago, and that makes me the happiest man on this side of the planet," Ken said, only to provoke him.

"Happy for you both," Brandon congratulated him, and he was suprised he did not care anymore about what the two of them did.

"Why aren't you angry? Or you've found some of those little girls to keep you company, and you've forgotten all about your dear wife."

Ken's revelation didn't affect Brandon. He had expected to feel angrier on meeting him, but he felt pity for him. He was rugged, thinner, and he didn't look like the happiest man he was claiming to be.

"Oh, that reminds me. Did you pay me a little visit last Thursday?" Brandon asked, looking for any clue, just to see if he was the one who had broken into Gera's room.

Ken seemed to have no idea.

"Why should I do that when I have a wife and a baby boy to keep me busy?" Ken asked innocently.

"Why shouldn't you?" Brandon wondered out loud.

Ken roared with laughter. "Maybe you are being haunted."

He then moved towards his white Toyota Corolla, leaving Brandon staring after him.

But never mind—Brandon was ready to tackle whatever puzzle Ken had in mind.

***

Two months went by faster than Brandon had expected. On the morning of his acquisition, he was very nervous. He knew this was a big task bestowed upon his shoulders. He found Gera looking at him curiously as he paced the sitting room, probably wondering what had him worked up. He heard her soft footsteps approaching and didn't turn around, just waited.

When she had reached him, she softly massaged his shoulders. He closed his eyes as the tension in him ebbed away. She then held him from behind and laid her head on his back. Did this woman know the effect she was having on him by holding him like that?

He slowly turned around so that he was facing her. Gera was becoming more beautiful each day, and he just couldn't resist noticing. Today, she wore a frilly cotton pink dress that hugged her soft curves.

"Don't be nervous. Everything is going to work out just right. You'll see," she convinced him, looking at him with those coffee brown eyes he'd come to love so much.

"Thank you," he whispered. "It's just that what is worrying me is more than the acquisition, Gera. So much more."

"What is it about? Please tell me," she pleaded.

"Will you help me?" he asked.

"If I knew what it was, it would be easy to know the answer to that, don't you think?"

"A week from now, we are going for a team-buiding vacation together with my new employees," he told her.

"And?" she asked, sounding impatient already.

"Everyone will be coming with their wives, and I am very worried about myself. I am going to be bored. Imagine a whole two weeks," he finished off, and he saw her understand what had him so worried.

"So you want someone to go with you, right?" she asked.

"Exactly! I wanted to ask you, but I didn't know how you were going to respond. Gera, I want you and me to pretend for these two weeks that we are husband and wife."

She seemed surprised and didn't respond for a while.

"Gera, please say something," he pleaded with her.

Her surprise turned into a wicked smile. "You know everything comes at a price, dear, and this isn't an exception."

He knew she was flirting and decided to join in the game. Nothing to lose.

"What price do you have in mind? Is it something I can handle?" he asked, winking at her and giving her the once-over.

Gera looked away, scratching her head, and it made him give her one of his sweetest smiles.

"Of course, it's money. Did you have another thing in mind, dear Brandon?" she replied, smiling, probably liking the look of disappointment on his face now.

"I thought it was something more valuable than money. But money, it is," he countered. "How much, to be precise?"

"Five thousand shillings a day isn't much to ask for. You can handle that, can't you?" she asked, tracing her index finger on his chest. As his muscle flexed under her touch, she smiled. "Just returning the favour," she said, looking at him in the eyes.

"Ok, five thousand. I hope you are worth it."

"You know that doesn't include the extras, if you know what I mean," she said smugly.

On these words, she went out of his room to prepare breakfast. Brandon looked at her departing form, and with that body, she was worth more than every penny in his bank account.

He had to admit that he had allowed unholy pictures of Gera in his mind. How would she be in bed? Would she be a smooth or rough rider? Would she scream loudly or stifle the moan? How would she look without those clothes on? This woman just had a way of playing with his libido.

The sun was rising from the horizon, casting its golden rays across the sky that it illuminated, making it look spectacular, as always. He smiled at the sunrise because Gera had just solved one of his major problems.

***

Brandon came out of his room and sat down at the kitchen table where breakfast was already set.

"Where is Gera? Oh! Sorry, I meant Loiser!" he asked, surprised.

"Seems you can't get me out of your mind, can you?" Gera told him, smiling, her lips forming a pout.

His gaze landed on her lips before he looked away distractedly.

"Seems so," he replied.

"Loiser is behaving strangely these days. She has already left."

"I'll see what is bothering her," he told her, then finished off his breakfast and stood up to leave.

"Success in everything," she told him.

"Thank you very much," he told her. He went to her and hugged her tightly. She felt so good in his arms, and he closed his eyes to savour the moment, wishing that it would last forever. "Can I receive a good luck kiss?"

"Don't you think you are asking for too much today? she told him, winking.

"Okay, you can have it your way. See you later," he told her and started for the door.

"Oh, I didn't know that you give up that easily, my dear Brandon," she challenged.

He glanced at his watch, saw he only had thirty minutes. He turned around and walked purposefully towards her and stopped right in front of her. Gera must then have figured out she was in trouble.

He didn't make a move, just watched like this were a movie. She took another step, and now, their bodies were brushing.

She seemed to gather her courage, put her hands around his neck, and pulled his head down so that his mouth could meet hers. He did not offer any resistance or assistance. She coaxed him to open his mouth to her with her tongue as she gently caressed his head with her hands.

At this, he abandoned his cool and responded to the kiss eagerly. The kiss was so full of intensity that when it was over, they were both panting.

Gera's lips were swollen now. And she looked so vulnerable that he was almost sure that if he pleaded his case, they would be behind some closed door and windows. But he didn't want their first time to be rushed. He wanted to savour her body and worship at her feet all night long, at least.

"That's the best success kiss I have ever received. I have to go, or else ..." he said as he went out of the door, whistling.

He was going to be late, but who really cared? He was the boss, and he couldn't be late. Maybe the others had just arrived early. He drove like the devil was on his heels, not wanting to remember the kiss because he was afraid he might as well turn the car and head home to Gera.

When he got to Soar Company, everything was ready. Tom Otieno greeted him as he took the seat next to his.

"What took you so long, Mr. Odhiambo? Need I ask why your eyes are glowing like that?"

Tom chuckled under his breath, and Brandon only gave him an acknowledging smile.

Tom was the former owner of the Soar Company. The group of workers he was supposed to work with looked uptight. All ties, serious looks, and Brandon just wondered how their lives were. Boring was the word he found. Was that the existence he really wanted? Gera had once told him that if you take life too serious, you might never come out of it alive.

The handing-over ceremony took a shorter time than he had expected. Later, they were mingling. He didn't like the employees on the spot, but he didn't have any valid reason. He was going to make them work on his terms. If they could not work to his satisfaction, then he would fire them and remain with those willing to work according to his policies. He was here in flesh, but his mind was back at the house with Gera.

What was she doing at the moment?

Chapter Nine

Gera was in her room working on a drawing. This was a hobby she had developed while still in primary school. She could draw the plants, trees, and buildings vividly using pencil on paper. When she joined high school, she would draw her classmates at a fee of two-hundred Kenyan shillings. She would use this money as pocket money and save the extra.

Loiser rapped at her door, peeping through the open doorway, and she beckoned her in. When Gera saw that she was focusing on the picture she had drawn, she quickly stashed it away. That only served to pique Loiser's interest. The girl smiled mischieviously at her and started tickling her until Gera couldn't laugh anymore.

"Stop it! I am going to show you the drawing, but not until you tell me what's been bothering you."

Loiser paused for a while before nodding.

Gera retrieved the picture and gave it to her. Loiser looked at it in amazement.

"Wow! I didn't know that you can draw. I love it," she said, smiling affectionately at her as she traced her hand on drawing.

"Thank you."

"You love him, don't you?" Loiser asked, looking at her expectantly.

Gera was thrown off balance for a while, and Loiser laughed.

"You think I haven't noticed? I have never seen my father this happy, Gera. You give him a reason to smile."

She just smiled, wondering how Loiser had grown up so fast.

She held the girl's hand and looked her in the eyes. "I don't know if I love him, but I know that I like him a lot."

"If you feel like loving him, don't hesitate. You have all my support. Imagine you being my mother. I'll be the happiest girl in the whole wide world."

When Gera looked at her face brimming with excitement, she knew that Loiser was sincere.

"Thanks. But let's not get ahead of ourselves. So what's been bothering you, dear?"

Loiser knotted her hands in her lap. "There's this girl in my class called Elsie. She has a group of girls that cling to her like leeches. They saw me talking to this handsome boy in my class called Stanley, and they approached me and warned me to stay far away from him."

"A handsome boy?" Gera asked, lowering her voice conspiratorily.

Loiser looked up at her, her eyes wide, and she softly nodded.

"Loiser, come on. Tell me more about him."

"You don't mind that I have a crush on a boy?"

"No! It means that you are becoming a big girl. It should not be something shameful. In fact, it is beautiful."

Loiser's face beamed as her smile widened. "He is on the second row while I am on the first row. Recently, I have caught him on several occasions staring at me. I look away, but when I look back at him, he is still staring. He is always quiet and reserved. He is the most handsome boy in our class, and girls are always flocking around him, but he doesn't pay them attention. He always smiles and moves away. Last week, he sat next to me during lunch, and we talked."

"What did you talk about?"

"Nothing interesting. The usual school stuff. During games, Elsie and her gang approached me behind the school computer room and threatened me with a knife."

"Did you report them to the headteacher?"

Loiser shook her head violently. "I can't do that."

"Why?"

"I will become the laughingstock of the class. I just have to avoid Stanley."

When she was through, Gera was furious.

"How dare they do that?" She then patted Loiser on the back. "Consider the problem solved."

***

The next day, they went to her school, and Gera asked Loiser to show her Elsie and her gang. She waited when they were going out of the gate in the evening and caught sight of the posse. They were six girls, and Gera understood just why Loiser was afraid of them. They walked like they owned the school, and most of the girls in Loiser's class kept their distance.

Elsie was the most beautiful of the six, and from what Gera had gathered, her father was an ambassador. But so what? That didn't give her the right to harass others just because she was born with a silver spoon in her mouth.

Elsie was in front, modeling and swinging her hips in a provocative manner. Gera was just at the gate waiting. When Elsie got nearer, she put her foot forward so that Elsie stumbled on it and fell. The other members of the gang went to her rescue, and Gera was impressed—such loyalty. Elsie got a few bruises on her elbow, but the bigger mess was on her spotless face.

When Elsie got up on her two feet, she looked hard at Gera and went charging at her. *Bingo*. Gera aimed at her wrapper games skirt and tagged at it. The next thing they knew, Elsie was naked, and Gera had her skirt. Elsie was so embarrassed because many boys, especially Stanley, were watching the show.

"What do you want?" Elsie asked between sobs. She had always seemed so high and mighty that nothing bad could catch up with her. "I am going to tell my father," she went on, and the others jeered, Loiser included.

"Why don't you apologize to Loiser for threatening her with a knife before I give you back your skirt, unless you enjoy walking naked," Gera told her, smiling.

Elsie seemed defiant at first, but then, she saw the others looking at her, like they were really pitying her while many were enjoying her fall.

"Loiser, come here," Gera called out. Loiser went forward, and Elsie looked at her menacingly, baring her teeth.

"I'm sorry for threatening you with a knife because of Stanley," she said, as if the words were choking her. The other pupils were silent for a minute, listening to her apology.

"Apology accepted," Loiser said at last.

Gera gave her back her skirt, which she took eagerly and quickly wrapped around her.

The audience disappeared, seeing that there was no more juicy show. Elsie ran from the scene as fast as her legs could carry her. Gera gave Loiser a wink, and they held hands as they went home.

"Thanks, partner in crime," Loiser told her as they walked in silence.

The sun was setting on the horizon, casting its golden rays in the sky, marking the end of yet another day.

***

"Hey girls, where have you been?" Brandon asked them when they arrived.

Gera looked at Loiser conspiratorily and turned to him. The two gave him broad smiles he'd never seen on them, and he knew he was out of the secret.

"You must tell me what's going on," he went on.

"Catch us if you can," Gera and Loiser chorused as they ran up the stairs.

If the two thought they were being clever, then he was going to prove them wrong.

He went after them at full speed thinking he could catch up with them. When he got upstairs, all was quiet. He didn't even know which room they got into. He searched Loiser's room, but they were nowhere to be seen, and they were not in Gera's room, either.

He then went to look for them in his room. It took him some time before he heard some movements in his wardrobe. He smiled to himself, went to check inside, looked under the bed, but didn't find them. Where were they? He stood, intending to listen for another sound. Maybe the first one was just some rats or his imagination playing tricks on him.

It appeared Loiser couldn't contain herself anymore, and her giggling drew his attention to the top of wardrobe, from where he saw the two dames looking at him. He smiled at them and just wondered how they'd gotten up there so fast. The chuckling grew to laughter, then they all guffawed out loud.

"Okay, I surrender," he admitted at last.

***

Brandon had already prepared supper and the evening tea. They all sat at the table enjoying the tea.

If I get married one day, I'd like to get a husband like Brandon, Gera thought to herself as she silently sipped from her mug, looking at Brandon who was lost in his eating.

That realization came to her as a suprise. As a young girl, she had always visualized herself having a big wedding and happy thereafter, but that dream had been lost somewhere.

As if Brandon, too, was having the same thoughts, he looked up at her, and she quickly glanced away when she realized she had been caught staring. He smiled at her and quickly turned to Loiser; it seemed she was in her own world.

He then announced their trip to his daughter. A mischievious smile played on her lips upon hearing of the trip, and it appeared Brandon just had to ask why she was smiling.

"Can I go and stay at Jane's place while you are gone?" Loiser asked enthusiastically. Jane was her best friend, and she knew they were going to have fun together. Gera saw the way her eyes lit with the idea, and she knew Brandon couldn't just refuse. After all, it was only for a while.

"Alright, you can stay there, but dear, don't cause them trouble," he told her lovingly.

"I swear I'll be on my best behavior, Dad. I know you will also have a good time," Loiser told them both.

Chapter Ten

The next two days fled like the devil was on their heels. The D-Day was here, a bright Saturday morning. Loiser's bags were already packed, as well as those of Brandon and Gera. Loiser offered to pray, and it went like, "Oh, God, protect my father and Gera. Bless them. Let them do only good things. Protect me, too. Amen."

Gera and Brandon broke into laughter.

He drove to Jane's place where they bade Loiser goodbye.

He had been observing everything from the side mirror. At first, he had thought it was just some random vehicle, but when he halted at the road side, the black Toyota also stopped but at a safe distance. He wasn't fooled—he knew better. He reversed the car so fast that his pursuer didn't have time to run away. He caught up with the car and even knocked its lights out.

Ken got out of his car, angrily cursing. "You thick-headed bastard! How dare you?"

"Oh, so it is you again," Brandon responded cooly.

"You bastard, you are going to pay dearly," Ken threatened.

"If you get anywhere near Loiser, I swear on my grandmother's grave that you are not going to live to see another day," Brandon told him, looking him dead in the eye to ensure that the message was well delivered.

He saw surprise in Ken's eye and just wondered how dumb the man could be sometimes. With that message home, he got into his car and drove up to where Ken was still rooted to the ground. He rolled down the car window. "Remember what I told you."

Gera eyed him worriedly, probably wondering about what had transpired. He looked ahead and kept driving, too angry to answer any question.

He was lost in his thoughts and nearly collided with a trailer. It was that fool's fault that he was now very worried about Loiser.

"What's wrong?" Gera asked him tenderly as she moved closer to him on the seat.

He parked the car beside the road after slowing down. Gera massaged his taut neck and shoulder to ease his stress away. It took some time before he spoke. He, on the other hand, was enjoying her tender hands on his skin, working their magic on him. How could just the touch of her hands have such an effect on him?

"I think we should bring Loiser along. I don't trust that man one bit, and I can't forgive myself if something bad happens to her. I can't," he spoke at last.

"Then let's go and bring her with us. I know she would be happy to tag along," Gera told him, smiling like that had been her thoughts all along, too.

He reversed the car and drove to Jane's place at full speed. Loiser and Jane were already playing outside with their dolls.

Loiser asked them why they had returned almost immediately. They explained that they were taking her for the trip. Brandon talked to Jane's mother, who nodded in agreement. Loiser quickly went inside the house and picked her bag.

Within no time, the three of them were on the road again. Brandon saw it fit for Loiser to miss classes for two weeks but be safer with them than for her to wind up dead or injured. He knew Ken was far more dangerous than he dared to admit.

***

The journey was long, but they didn't even notice. They sang songs and made up stories, making the trip even more enjoyable. At lunch time, they were in Nairobi, and they stopped at Villa Rosa Kempinsky for lunch. They received a warm welcome and smiles from the hotel security persons as they got to the entrance.

Gera could not help but notice the beautiful sculptures at the front of the hotel with their fountains of water overflowing rhythmically. The aroma of the exotic food met them as they walked in.

"Wow!" Loiser exclaimed as she sat down. "This place is awesome, Dad. Look at the beautiful screens with beautiful pictures. I love it. It looks like Disneyland."

Brandon smiled at his daughter, loving her enthusiasm.

They had a buffet, first starting with the soup. The main course meal was so delicious. By the time they were on the dessert, they were full. He paid with his credit card, and they left. They drove for another five hours before they finally saw their destination, Blue

Springs Beach Hotel. Beyond the hotel, the sea waves washed the white sand, the whoosing sound soothing. It was a beautiful twilight. The three alighted, stretching their taut muscles.

It seemed the others had heard them arriving and came to welcome them. There were twelve employees, their wives, and their children. Loiser's eyes lit when she saw all the other seven kids. Within no time, the children had bonded and run off. The adults were left alone. Brandon introduced Gera as his wife. It felt so right to call her that.

***

Gera felt embarrassed at first because she knew they were deceiving these wonderful people. When she saw most of the women looking at her enviously, she decided that she just might as well go along with their ploy. Brandon held her at the small of her back as he led her to greet them, introducing each of them to her. She felt warm and safe in his hold.

"Is this really you, Gera?" a short, brown, beautiful woman exclaimed, and Gera turned to look at her.

"Rosie!" she exclaimed, too, as she went to greet her. They hugged for so long. The others just looked on as the two women embraced each other.

"Mmh, where did you catch this big fish? I hope I'll go fishing with you next time," Rosie whispered to her ear as they broke off their embrace.

Gera saw the wicked twinkle in her eyes and grinned, not believing that Rosie, her childhood friend from the Oyugis, was here. She squeezed her hand mouthing 'later' and went back to Brandon's side.

When they had gotten acquainted with everyone, he announced to them that they'll meet the next day, and they all disappeared to their rooms. The children had their rooms, separate from their parents'.

The room was magnificent. The roof was designed using the local makuti leaves, giving the space a beachy ambience. The walls were wooden and painted in white, the floor also wooden. The sitting room was superb, covered with chairs made of mahogany wood which had brown animal print cushions.

Being in the room alone made Gera feel in communion with nature. They had a radio with grand speakers, a wide screen TV. The kitchen was spotlessly clean. Their final place to tour was the bedroom, which had a serene atmosphere, with a red, upholstered four-poster bed in the middle of it. It had blue sheets and a flowery duvet neatly spread with matching pillows. The walls were covered with pictures of the sea at sunset and sunrise. It was so simple yet so beautiful.

She was so engrossed in her voyage that she forgot Brandon was in the room, too. He cleared his voice, startling her.

"So, what do you think?" he asked her as he drew the window curtains.

"Not much."

"That's why you took flight to Disneyland leaving me on Earth, I see," he reiterated.

She looked at him and smiled. He smiled back.

"Come here, my dear wife," he said, holding his hands out.

"Yes, my dear husband," she answered when she got near. "I'm at your service."

Brandon teased her, using her last statement to get to her. "Thank you again, Gera. Since you are at my service, why don't you start by undoing my shoe laces bacause these shoes are killing my feet."

They both laughed as he gave her a warm hug.

A rap at the door interrupted their embrace. He went to open and found that the waitress had brought them food. He set the table and called Gera. They ate their food in silence, the whole day's journey taking its toll on them. After supper, they showered in turns and prepared for bed.

"Where am I sleeping, husband?" she asked him.

"On the bed. That's where both husband and wife sleep," he told her.

She looked at him disapprovingly. "I'll be damned if I am going to sleep with you."

"But you are not going to sleep with me, although that's a wonderful idea. You are going to sleep beside me," he told her, smiling at her misunderstanding. "I'm too tired, so don't worry. I am going to sleep like a log."

With that assurance, she got into bed because she was too tired to continue with the argument whose end she couldn't even see. Brandon slipped in beside her. She moved towards the edge until she was almost falling down, which amused him.

"Oh, my. Gera, stop behaving like a virgin who has never slept beside a man," he told her, still laughing.

"Has it not occurred to you that I am behaving like this because I am one?" she countered angrily and immediately regretted even opening her mouth.

That statement killed his laughter instantly.
***

So what he had suspected all along was true? Gera was still a virgin.

"I'm sorry for that," he apologized.

"Are you sorry for me because I am still a virgin?" she asked, now turning to face him, and, oh boy, with that look where he knew he was in for it.

"I didn't mean that—"

He hadn't even finished making his statement before Gera pulled the duvet to her side, leaving him cold.

So that was it? Gera covered herself with the whole duvet, leaving only her head, and she smiled sweetly at him. An idea planted itself in his mind. He moved closer to her, too close for comfort now.

"Just trying to get heat," he replied to her unasked question.

"You goat! Take your share of the blanket and get away from me."

Brandon took his part of the blanket and went to sleep.

Chapter Eleven

The next day, Brandon woke up long before the sun came up. Gera was dead asleep, and he had all the time in the world to stare at her. She looked peaceful and serene in her sleep. Just looking at her like this made him realize that he loved her even more than he deemed possible. He was tempted to kiss her. Why shouldn't he? He moved closer to her, and she didn't even stir.

"Don't do it, please!" Gera screamed from her sleep, startling him from his original plan.

"Gera! Wake up!"

He shook her from her sleep, and she woke up with a start. He pulled her to him so that he could comfort her. Gera held onto him for her dear life, resting her head on his chest.

She started shaking violently, and he thought she was crying. She gave a loud laugh as she pulled a way from him. The truth then dawned on him.

"You wicked woman!" he said, smiling at her. He had thought she was truly having a nightmare, when in reality, she had just been pulling some trick on him. Gera never failed to amaze him each and every time.

He retrieved a pillow from his back and hit her with it. She took hers to defend herself. Before long, they were running about the room pillow-fighting.

Brandon always felt uptight, but since Gera had come into his life, he was becoming more carefree and laidback. Maybe Shaggy was right, after all, when he sang about the 'Strength of a woman.'

"That is enough, Brandon. I'm tired," she announced after some time.

They both fell on the bed, exhausted from their game. What a way to start a day! he wondered as he turned to look at her. He held out his right hand, and she put her soft hand into his rather rough one.

Their fingers entertwined as they looked deep into each other's eyes, none of them being able to break the gaze. It seemed their eyes were communicating the only language known to them, that of love. Even if no one was acknowledging it, it was there, and it was always going to loom around 'til they accepted the feeling for what it was.

***

Brandon went out to greet the sun and see what the others were up to. The sea breeze bathed his body as he stood by the shore, the morning sun warming him.

The expanse of the sea was comforting. The emptiness gave the impression of no past, no future, just the present at your disposal to manipulate. He was interested in the present, especially when it involved Gera.

He was so deeply absorbed in his inner thoughts that he didn't even see the joggers until they got nearer to him.

"Lazy bones, join us!" Joseph called out.

They were about ten joggers. From the way they were sluggishly jogging, they seemed worn out.

Brandon knew that this was not their everyday cup of tea, but he had to admire their effort. Looking at Philip who was fat and had a protruding stomach, you would think he was due to give birth any moment—it brought a smile to Brandon's mouth.

He joined them. Philip was faster than he had anticipated. With that body, you would be deceived that he was slower, but he was more agile than Brandon had thought.

When they were on the last miles, Philip shocked them all by emerging the first one. Brandon came second.

"Congrats, bro," came the praises from the other joggers.

Philip just looked at them and smiled, exposing his perfectly white teeth. Each of them had a dip in the sea water to wash away the sweat before going to breakfast.

***

Gera was busy with sketching the expanse of the sea. She could not quite capture the image of the waves as they kissed the white sands. She was lost in her thoughts watching the waves when she heard the door open. She turned around and found Brandon rooted to the spot, looking past her to the sketch she was making.

"Husband, what is wrong? You don't like my drawing?" she asked, concern creeping to her voice.

He just stood there, not responding. There was a long stretch of silence before he cleared his throat and stormed back into the room.

What the heck was wrong with him? She was tempted to follow him to get the answers to her questions, but her feet got stuck to the ground.

She wrapped her drawing equipments and went back to the room to store them. Today, she was dressed in a pair of white shorts, pink T-shirt, and a cape, and she was feeling as sexy as she looked. She found Brandon standing by the wide transparent glass window facing the ocean. He didn't even flinch when she got into the room.

She placed her drawing in a corner then sat on the bed. He turned to look at her, and she looked back at him. Their gaze held for a while before he broke it.

He then spoke for the first time since entering the room, his gaze still outside. "Why didn't you tell me that you draw?"

At first, she wanted to counter by saying that it was not part of her obligation to him whatever she did. But one look at him told her he was damn serious.

"I didn't think that it was important to you," she said instead.

That seemed to touch a cord because he took his eyes off the window and looked at her.

She couldn't understand what it was that had made him this angry. She was still contemplating what could have caused his anger when he started moving towards her. Without thinking, she got up on her feet and started backing off. He stopped short in his tracks and smiled.

"Why are you running away, Gera? You think that I am going to beat you? I have never even laid a hand on a woman."

She then realized her foolishness, but with that determined look on his face, and her being the focus, she just had to run.

"Come here," he commanded.

She timidly went to him. He held out his hand, and she put hers into his and then sat down on the bed, beside him. He didn't speak for a while, giving her time to relax.

"I didn't mean to scare you, sorry," he said at last. She looked at him anxiously. "I am angry that you were just throwing your talent to the dogs without developing it fully," he continued.

"What makes you think so?" she asked.

"Because you should search for opportunities such as exhibitions to sell your drawings and also to show the world your talent," he explained.

She frowned. "So you think money is everything. I don't care about money. There are a lot of things much more important than money."

His face lit up. "Like what?"

She looked at him. "Like being happy. Just being happy and finding that haven called happiness. Happiness is the essence of life. Without it, life is dead. The moment you find that place, you will always be alive, and that, dear husband, is something money cannot buy."

"I hadn't thought of life like that, you know. Now that you explained, it makes a little sense," he said. "Let me connect you with the most brilliant exhibitors so that you can show them your work. Maybe I haven't complimented you. I think you have a great potential."

"Don't worry, I don't need your help," she answered, her anger flaring.

She stood up and left the room. Who did he think he was? Some guardian angel sent to deliver her from distresss? Men could sometimes be stupid. Always searching for opportunities to chip in! Damn them all!

She went to the beach to get some fresh air. Since she'd seen Rosie, her brain had been wondering aimlessly to the past. She allowed the flashes of memories she had locked tightly to surface.

Brandon was suggesting that she put her drawings up for exhibition. Maybe he had a point. It was high time she started thinking seriously about her life. She had left home to look for that place called happiness. Yes, she had found it in Brandon's house, but she felt empty inside. She wanted more. She wanted something bigger than her, because what if something happened and she was forced to leave his house? Where would she go?

"I can see you are daydreaming," Rosie said, interrupting her thoughts.

Rosie wore a green sundress. She was so pretty that she reminded Gera of a doll. Gera greeted her and invited her for a walk on the beach. They talked about their childhood days. Gera also asked many questions about her relatives since she only had vague memories of her uncles and aunts. She wanted her roots back. She was sadly informed by Rosie that her uncles had shared their two hectares' piece of land among themselves after her family had left, and that only meant that she had nothing to go back to.

"Where did you proceed to after you left?" Rosie asked enthusiastically.

Gera just stared at her as if she had not heard her question. She was reliving that day when her uncles had thrown them out after her father's burial. They had left with their clothes as their only possession, had cried for mercy, but had received none. Gera's mother had not been married officially according to the Luo customs, so the uncles claimed that the marriage was not binding.

During the early stages in her stay at the orphanage, she had always dreaded that maybe something had happened to her mother. Maybe they had an accident and she had been seriously injured or died in the process. The thoughts had filled her with dread, and she would sit in a corner and bury her head in her lap and cry. She would pray for God to protect her mother or rest her soul in peace. She would imagine her mother watching and smiling at her and Queen from Heaven, and then the pain would be bearable.

However, she imagined this other possibility that her mother was of good health and living her life happily. The thought had always filled her with red rage.

One day, Mama Jane had called her and Queen to the office. When they'd arrived, they had found a tall, thin woman whose skin was pale, in a faded *Kitenge* dress. At first, Gera hadn't recognized her, but her face had been oddly familiar. When recognition had dawned on her, she had taken slow steps behind as if her legs were made of lead.

"No!" she had shouted and stumbled on a chair, landing on the ground with a thud, hissing when her buttocks connected with the cold hard concrete.

Mrs. Okumu had found her daughters all grown up, so much so that she could barely recognize them. She had expected them to run to her and embrace her.

"Gera and Queen, come here," she'd beckoned, her arms wide open.

Gera had looked at the open arms and had been reminded of a cold, deep abyss that was going to pull her in, swallowing her. Queen had looked at her apprehensively and had then gone to embrace their mother. Gera had watched them from her spot on the ground, not moving.

When the embrace had been over, they'd both had tears in their eyes, and her mother had rubbed Queen's back soothingly.

She'd wished she had tears to shed, but her eyes had remained dry as bones. She had gotten up from the ground slowly, her joints aching. How many times had she dreamt of this event? But it was thirteen years too late. Queen had stood beside their mother, in support, two against one, it had seemed.

"What do you want?" she'd asked, glaring at her mother.

"I have come to take you home."

"This is our home."

"Gera, please be kind. It's not like I abandoned you. I have come back for you," Mrs. Okumu had said.

Gera had snorted, not believing her ears.

"Mrs. Okumu. I believe that's your name. You left us here thirteen years ago, if I may jog your memory. You never came to visit us, not even once. Now, you have come out of the blue to claim that you want us back. You must be kidding," she had told her, feeling all the abandonment of thirteen years taking their toll on her.

Mrs. Okumu had flinched, as if in pain.

"Gera, where are your manners? I have always been thinking of you. It was just that I could not find time to come and see you. I did not have the fare to come to Kisumu every now and then. However, I prayed for you every night, for God Almighty to protect you. At least, I deserve appreciation for all the prayers. I can see that you are both fine and of good health," she had said, holding Queen's hand and extending the other to hold Gera's.

Gera had looked at the hand suspiciously—one would think it was a cobra waiting to strike her. Mrs. Okumu had dropped her hand and stepped back.

"Gera, please don't be like this," Queen had pleaded, tears trickling down her cheeks.

"Queen, she abandoned us here. She can't expect us to accept her with open arms."

"But she is our mother, and she has apologized," she'd gone on stubbornly.

"True, go ahead and forgive her. Count me out," Gera had said, storming out of the room.

She had sat by the pavement, staring into thin air, her mind a battlefield of thoughts.

"Gera," Mama Jane had called out, startling her. "Sorry."

Mama Jane had sat beside her, not speaking.

"What should I do?"

"It is not my place to say."

"What would you do, if you were in my shoes?"

She'd looked at the children playing on the swings and said, "I would give her a chance."

"No."

Mama Jane had shrugged. "Queen really wants to go with her. You can go with them, and if things don't work out, you are welcome to come back."

"I will think about it. I just need time."

"That's fine, but don't think for too long," she'd said, softly squeezing her shoulder.

The roaring of the ocean brought Gera back to reality. She could not bring herself to tell Rosie about her sufferings. It was too painful, and she was not ready to speak about it. She just wanted to live in her make-believe world and enjoy it while it lasted.

When Rosie saw how her question had put Gera in a pensive mood, she let it pass and changed the topic, telling Gera she was single. Gera could not believe it. Rosie was so pretty and lovable.

"Don't be deceived. Looks alone cannot make a man stick with you long enough to marry you. Men of today are not just the marrying type. All they want is to dip their hand into the cookie jar, and before you know it, they'll be fading away in the distance," Rosie told her, and she had to laugh.

"You have an inverted version of men," she said, and Rosie shook her head in disbelief.

"Maybe I could do with some pieces of advice. Don't I just love your man! He is tall, dark, and handsome. And with those thighs and able hands, I bet he makes you fly to the skies and back," Rosie said dreamily.

Gera could not help but laugh. If only Rosie knew that she and Brandon had not even made love. She knew that Brandon was handsome, but hearing it from Rosie made her feel very lucky to have him. She wanted to hold onto him tightly.

Her phone rang, Brandon's name lighting the screen. She received the call and heard his voice pleading, "Darling, it's not wise to leave your husband unattended for this long. I have missed you very much. Come back."

Heat crept up all over her body.

"I bet we'll catch up later so that you can share with me the bliss of marriage," Rosie announced when she saw Gera blushing from head to toe.

Chapter Twelve

Brandon was sipping his beer, listening to 'Skol' of Koffi Olomide, when his phone rang. He looked at the screen and immediately knew it was Jackie. Why was she calling? He ignored the first two calls. When she persisted with the calling, he had no choice. Maybe it was an emergency. He picked up the phone.

"Hello, Jackie. How are you?"

"Brandon, cut the pleasantries. I have something very important to tell you. You have to listen to me carefully."

He heard the urgency in her voice and obeyed. He had never heard her speak like that in all the years they were together.

"Go on," he urged.

"He is coming for your blood," she broke the news.

"Who is coming for my blood?" he asked, already fearing the answer.

"Silly! Ken is coming there either tomorrow or the day after tomorrow. Be prepared," she advised.

He had to laugh.

"Jackie, is this your ploy to trap me again? Sorry, but it won't work, so you better stop," he warned her.

"Brandon, listen. Trapping you sounds so enticing, but you have to believe me. I'm serious. Be careful," she said, then the line went dead.

He placed the phone on the table absent-mindedly, sipped his beer, but all of a sudden, it had lost its taste. Ken didn't always know when to stop. He had already taken Jackie from him three years ago, but that wasn't enough. He had wanted to hurt Loiser, too, some days back.

What? A thought came to his mind. Ken's plan had been to ensure that all of Brandon's family was in one place. This was because it was going to be easier to destroy them. How could he have been so foolish? He thought of something bad happening to Loiser or Gera and felt a knot form in his thoat.

He had two options—running away, or staying and fighting. The option of running away was the easy way out. Just go to a new place and start all over again. Problem was, he was going to keep running every time Ken knew of their location. He had to stay and fight and get it over with.

He was still weighing his options when Loiser came running into the room, her face beaming. She was in her blue swimming costume and dripping wet.

"Hi, Dad!" she called, going to her father for a hug.

"Hi, sweetheart. I have not seen you for a long time. What have you been up to?"

"I have been swimming with the other kids," she told him. "What about you?"

"As you can see, I'm not bored," he answered.

Gera entered the room, and Loiser ran to greet her. She giggled as she led Gera to the bar where Brandon was sipping his beer. Gera wore a white T-shirt and a pair of black shorts. Very sexy, he thought, giving her the elevator gaze.

He thought of losing the battle with Ken. He couldn't lose Gera and Loiser. He just couldn't.

"Geez, he isn't even listening," Loiser said.

They had been talking to him for the past minute, it seemed, but he had been in another world.

"Oh, sorry. I have a lot on my mind," he apologized. "What were you saying?"

"Is there something bothering you?" Gera asked, standing up to go to him.

"No, it is just that I have a lot on my plate today," he said nonchalantly.

"Let's drink," she said, bringing out more wine for them and Coke for Loiser. She poured red wine into her glass.

"What are we toasting to?" she asked, raising her glass.

"To happy life," Loiser said cheerfully.

"To happy life it is," Brandon concurred, and they toasted.

They drank as they talked, and time seemed to fly.

"Let's dance, everybody," he suggested.

Loiser stood up, already upbeat, but Gera remained seated.

"No, don't look at me. Two left feet," she replied.

Loiser went to tickle her so that she could get up, and that did the trick. *Oh, so that's it*, he thought, raising his eyebrows, knowing he would need the ploy some day.

Gera narrowed her eyes at him and whispered, "Don't you dare."

He turned the music up, and in no time, they were dancing the evening away. All the inhibitions left behind, he was showing them the moves he had learnt from college. And they laughed, clapped, and cheered him on.

Next, it was Loiser's turn to show them the latest choreographies, and he and Gera were awed. Kids nowadays had severe moves. She was throwing her hands in the air, jumping and moving around the floor every two seconds. Brandon observed that unlike the olden days when the slower you danced, the better, this young generation was the complete opposite.

"Your turn," Loiser shouted on top of the music.

Gera got on the floor and did the dance of her life. She was dancing slowly to the music, swaying her hips from side to side. Brandon couldn't keep his cool anymore. The way she was dancing revealed to him so much more than she would have ever shown during the other times. He saw vigour, passion, and determination.

He swallowed, his heartbeat picking speed. He looked at the seat Loiser had been occupying, but it was empty. When had she left?

***

Gera was so lost in dance that she didn't even notice Brandon moving towards her. She only noticed when her back was against his broad chest and felt his warm breath down her neck. She stopped dancing, but the music rolled on. Her heart raced as she waited. She could also feel the hammering of his heart on her back.

He tenderly kissed her shoulder, inching up onto her neck, planting small, feather-like kisses but leaving a whole swarm of tingling sensation in their wake.

He continued giving her the small doses of kisses. On reaching her ear, he took it hungrily into his mouth like it was a delicious meal, and she moaned. That alone broke off the string of composure he'd seemed to be hanging onto. He swung her around, and their lips collided. He kissed her ferociously, without any restraint—he let it all out.

He was a little bit rough with her, but she let him. She, too, wanted to feel the intensity, relish in it, and embrace it. She was ready to throw caution to the wind and let things take their course. Maybe this was destiny.

A rap came at the door, and all the sensuality melted into thin air. Maybe this wasn't destiny, after all.

"Sorry," Philip apologized, looking from Brandon to her. They stood close, heaving. "Everyone is waiting by the fire. Join us."

"We'll be there in a minute," Brandon said distractedly, after clearing his throat.

Gera rushed to the bathroom to enable her nerves to cool down. She closed the door after her and leaned on it. She remembered the kiss, still fresh as paint in her head. She remembered the caresses, even fresher.

She bolted from the door to the mirror and was astonished by her appearance. Her hair was shaggy, her eyes bright, and her lips still swollen from the kiss. She had to stop this before it was too late.

Gera did not have to look to know that it was him when the door was flung open. She already knew that he would come to her. It was inevitable. At first, it had been just a wish, then hope, which evolved into a want and later a need. She turned to look at him. He was still standing at the door, each hand in his trousers' pockets. The pose reminded her of a warrior.

She pressed her thighs together, trying to quell the thrumming at her core.

One look into his eyes, and she was captivated by them. No matter how much she wanted to look away, she couldn't. She saw fire, desire, and something else she didn't understand. She felt scared. Not as scared as when she had found herself in the orphanage all alone, with the other children looking at her pitifully, mirroring their own feelings. Now, she was just afraid of the unknown.

Brandon's gaze scalded her flesh everywhere he looked.

"Make up your mind right now, Gera, because when I start, there is no stopping me," he whispered breathlessly.

She could not speak. She tried to open her mouth, but no words came out. She found herself shivering involuntarily. Brandon's long legs ate the distance between them in two strides, and he stopped right in front of her.

He looked into her eyes, desire dripping from his brown gaze like honey.

He tilted her chin tenderly upwards. "I'll be gentle, I promise."

She did not doubt his gentleness. The problem was, what about tomorrow? What if things didn't work out between them? She just knew that she'd be shattered.

He kissed her, and all the voices in her head disappeared. She put her hands around his neck, moved closer to him. He smelt so right. How could something that felt this right be wrong? If at all it was wrong, then she didn't want to be right.

The kissing became intense, then wild. She didn't know if she could continue standing. He swept her off her feet and carried her, heading to their bedroom.

On the way, she inched closer to his left ear, breathing heavily down his neck, and whispered, "I hope you are as good as you kiss."

He nearly stumbled, then looked at her tenderly. "Don't do that."

"Or else what?" she dared.

"I'll take you right here," he retorted and rushed to their room, easing her on the mattress.

He leaned in, and they resumed their kissing. He moved lower, caressing her breasts, and this made her moan in pleasure. He then took off her T-shirt, and her arms lifted up to cover her breasts.

"No," he said gruffly, tugging at her hands.

He took off his shirt, too. She looked at his chest and saw the muscles playing, and she traced the protruding veins and felt a shudder run through him. Brandon then proceeded to free her of her bra, but she was not giving in.

"Brandon, I—"

"Hush, my dear," he whispered.

He removed his jeans and pulled her shorts, exposing a pair of lacy, pink panties.

He groaned and tugged at her panties, leaving her bare to his inspection. His gaze travelled to hers, and she was tempted to cover herself when his eyes darkened with desire.

"Beautiful," he said, inching towards her sex.

When he got near, he parted her and inhaled her scent, closing his eyes.

Gera was now a squirming mass, shivering. When he blew on her sex, she jerked upwards away from him. He pulled her towards his open mouth and drank from her fountain. When his mouth connected with her core, she screamed.

"Please, Brandon, stop."

"Not yet," he said hoarsely before he resumed his ministrations.

He lapped at her juices which were now flowing, penetrating her with his tongue. She stretched her hands and held his head as it bobbed in and out, round and round, driving her to the stars. He sucked her clit into his warm mouth, nibbling while his digits parted her. She shuddered, and when he made a come-hither with his index finger, she crashed into a million pieces.

He looked up at her, and she shook her head, spent and well-satiated. He opened his wallet and removed a foil of protection, sheathing himself while eyeing her. Her eyes widened when she saw his impressive size. She licked her lips.

He lined himself with her entrance and pushed in. She was tight, and he had to inch in bit by bit. She hissed, breathing through her mouth.

"Sorry," he whispered when he was fully seated in her and she gave a yelp.

When he started moving slowly at first, she felt a dull ache overridden by pleasure. They looked into each other's eyes as they moved in unison. He increased the pace, and she rounded her hips, meeting him halfway. Beads of moisture formed on his face and whole body, dripping onto her already sweaty body. He leaned forward and kissed her, riding her faster. Flesh slapping against flesh.

The tempo increased as they approached their climax, and they cried out their release in unison. Brandon then rolled onto his side and tightly held her, letting her head rest on his chest.

Gera felt loved and cherished like never before. She peeked up and found him looking at her. She had never been looked at with so much love. He then planted small kisses on her face and a big one on her lips. She wanted to keep this memory forever. After a while, he picked her up again.

"Where are we going?" she asked.

"I'm going to take care of you."

***

When they reached the bathroom, he opened up the shower, and warm water sprinkled onto their bodies. He took the soap and lathered it on her. She did the same for him. He smoothly caressed her body, giving every part the attention it deserved, blessing her body.

She then put her hands around his neck and asked, "Again?"

"I have barely started," he whispered in her ear.

They made love again with the shower running. This time, it was better and sweeter than the last. When they had finished, they bathed again. He then carried her to bed and held her so close.

"I love you," he started.

"Because we made love?" she asked, looking him straight in the eyes.

"No! You feisty woman! I have known for a while now. It's just that I didn't voice it out," he retorted, kissing her nose.

"Oh! That's good to know," she replied casually, yet inside, happiness seemed to be welling up.

Brandon suspected she was just playing hard to get. An idea came into his mind. Gera tried to escape, but she was too late. He inched his fingers towards her armpit, and he started tickling her. She jerked away, trying to escape, but he followed her, tickling her relentlessly. The sound of her laughter and giggles filled the room.

"Stop it, or else I'll wet myself," she pleaded.

"Not until you accept," he countered.

"Accept what, you bully?" she retorted, and that seemed to set him off again, and this time, she gave up and told him. "Okay! Stop it. I am telling you. I like you, I like you a lot."

He looked at her lovingly. Liking was more than enough for him at the moment. It had never mattered whether he was accepted or not, but at this very moment, he wanted to be loved, cherished by this very woman.

But he was not in a hurry. He was going to make Gera fall madly and deeply in love with him.

***

Brandon hugged her tightly, moulding her body to his.

"Can I ask you a question?" He moved just an inch from her so that he could see her face.

"Go right ahead, dear."

"I know that we have stayed with you for over a year now, but I know nothing about your past. I know that maybe I am asking for too much, but I just want to know," he said and almost regretted even opening his mouth.

Gera's face, which had been glowing a minute ago, turned pale, and big drops of tears trickled down her face.

"Holy Jesus!" he cursed and moved lower to kiss her tears away.

He soothed her until the crying stopped.

"You don't have to tell me if you don't feel like it," he said, still wondering what it was in the past that had hurt her that much. Some people might say that the past doesn't matter, but in the long run, it did, especially if it affected the present in any way.

"I prefer to live in the present because no matter how hard I try, there is no way I'm going to change the past. My past brings me lots of pain that I would not like to dwell on now," she said, looking ahead.

"It's alright," he said tersely. He was annoyed, but he didn't know why. He really understood her, but what hurt so much was that she didn't trust him enough to want to share her pain with him.

Gera eyed him apprehensively and sat up, knotting her hands in her lap. When he remained silent and sulking, she got off the bed, wrapping the white sheet around her body and headed for the sitting room.

He saw her going away and didn't blame her. While he was cursing her for not opening up to him, had he done the same? She also didn't know much about him, especially the issue of Jackie.

"Wait, Gera," he called before she had walked out the door.

She stopped and slowly turned to look at him, her eyes filled with sadness.

"For what?" she whispered.

He smiled his megawatt smile and tapped on the bed.

She just stood there looking at him, and for a moment, he thought she was going to walk out on him. When she started moving towards him, he breathed a sigh of relief.

He sat up and put her between his legs, and she did not resist. She rested her head on his shoulder, his three-day old beard tickling her cheek. A few days ago, things had been easy. Why did sex always complicate things? He knew that right now, he was a part of her, and she was a part of him. He couldn't just walk away without knowing whether she'll be fine or not.

"I'm sorry," he whispered to her.

"It's alright."

The matter could wait for another day. It was only that time was against him. Then he remembered Ken, and he felt his blood run cold in his veins. He was afraid of the future, and that's why he was impatient to know things fast. Just when he was starting over all over again, Ken wanted to destroy everything that really mattered to him. One thing was for sure, by the time all this was over, one of them would be dead. Chances were fifty-fifty. Tonight might be even the last with Gera, and that scared him.

"What's disturbing you, and don't lie to me, please?" she pleaded, caressing his beard. "You seemed very far away since yesterday. The only time you were really here was when you were making love to me."

Brandon was surprised. He had thought he had really well-concealed his worries, but he should have known better that nothing escaped the watchful eyes of Gera.

"It's nothing. I would not like to burden you with my problems."

"It doesn't seem like a small matter. I want to know what's going on, Brandon, please."

He knew he was in a fix. If he told her, she might panic, and if he did not, then it would even be difficult to protect her. He was still undecided on what to do when an idea came to his mind.

"I just want to ask you for one favour. I want you to take Loiser with you and go to my sister's place in Nairobi. Then I'll meet you there later," he requested and just wished that she would not question his intentions.

He saw it wise to send them to his sister, Elvin Achieng. She was an Administration Police Officer stationed in Lang'ata. He knew that at Lang'ata, they would be safer since to reach them, Ken would have to pass through the police officers.

"I have heard your requested, but don't you think that at least I deserve to know what's going on?"

"Gera, please just go. I will answer all your questions once this is all over," he told her, hoping that was enough explanation for Stubborn Gera.

"Is it something to do with Ken and Jackie?" She dived right into the heart of the issue.

"Yes," he said, clearing his throat.

For a moment, he had lost control and almost rebuked her for mentioning Jackie and opening unhealed wounds. He also saw the hurt in her eyes when she realized that it still hurt him that Jackie had left him for another man, a mighty blow to his ego. Where had these sensitive feelings hidden themselves for so long? Why were they popping their ugly heads when they were taking critical steps in their lives? He raked his mind but couldn't come up with a definite answer.

"I'm staying," she said finally.

"Don't even start," he told her, fearing that his imagination had become reality.

He had hoped and prayed that Gera would just concur with him this one time and leave. He did not want anything bad to happen to her.

"I have not even started, and don't think that you are going to talk me out of it," she warned him.

He just had to love her stubbornness.

It was what had attracted him first to her. It was what made her intriguing. It was what made her come alive. It was what she thrived on.

But where Ken was involved, it was going to get her killed. Brandon didn't even want to imagine what that would do to him.

"Gera, please listen to me, for once. Ken is mad, dangerous, and even murderous. He could hurt you, and that's his intention. I can't lose you. I love you too much, and it will break me into pieces. Just leave and take Loiser with you," he pleaded with her.

Chapter Thirteen

"You think it's only you who has feelings? I will also feel lost without you, lost like I was before I met you. Left in an orphanage, just because where my mother remarried, they did not want outcast children. My mother left me and my sister in a children's home all helpless, vulnerable, and teary. She did not care about us, only her happiness.

"Brandon, I felt so alone. I don't want to feel that way again. Please don't make me go through it again," Gera said, tears flowing like from a broken well.

She was shaking so violently that he held her like a baby, just as he would have held that child who had been left at the orphanage.

He had wanted to know about the past, had even gotten angry when the answers hadn't been forthcoming. But now, he even regretted asking. It was so selfish of him to want her to relive those dark moments of the past.

"Make love to me," she whispered in his ear, and it was the least he could do to her for the damage he had caused. Sadness had a way of playing with emotions.

When he kissed her, she pulled him close, deepening the kiss. Her tongue tangled with his, and a whimper escaped her mouth. He reached between her legs to find her dripping wet for him. He groaned as he eased his index finger and she begged, "Please, Brandon, now."

He wished he could hold this out a little longer, but he wasn't that strong. He was sporting a hard-on that she was frantically working in her fist.

He positioned her on all fours and guided his shaft to her entrance, teasing her, pushing the head and withdrawing before moving in half-way. He finally inched all the way in, stuffing her, and she sighed. Then, he started moving, picking up speed, holding her hip in place as he thrust in and out of her.

"Faster, Brandon," she whispered breathlessly, and he pumped into her harder, chasing his own release.

She shuddered, heaving, and he rubbed her back before quickening his pace. Sweat dripping from his body, he groaned as he poured his seed into her.

"Did I hurt you?" he asked breathlessly.

"Yes, so much," she replied jokingly. "It's getting better by the minute."

How could she joke when danger was just a heartbeat away? And this made him love her even more.

Outside, the Indian Ocean's waves were lapping at the white sand. The sun was also casting its golden rays into the dark sky, lighting it up, coming from below the water line. It was morning again. A new beginning in their lives.

They fell asleep, bone tired.

Brandon was the first to stir awake, and he admired sleeping Gera. He counted himself a lucky man to have the love of this woman. He rolled out of bed and went to prepare them some breakfast. He made tea, toasted bread, and poured some juice into a glass jug.

It was so long since he had done that. Back then, it had been for Jackie ... Why did the thought of Jackie lately pop into his thoughts? He carried the tray into the bedroom and found Gera already up.

"I didn't know you could get so romantic," she teased, sitting up.

"I can get more romantic than this. Just try me," he teased back, winking at her, and she blushed.

He laughed at her. "You still blush. Oh, my!"

"Don't be so sure of yourself. It was not for you."

He fed her breakfast, and she fed him him in return. They both wished the moment would last forever, and if not in this life, then in the next.

***

Gera sat on the bed, anxiously waiting for Brandon to come back. He had gone to check on Loiser thirty minutes ago, and he was taking awfully long to return. Had he found her? Were they fine, or had something happened to them? Her uneasiness however coud not allow her to sit still and wait for the worst to happen. She went to the window to look, out but did not catch any sign of Brandon or Loiser. Something was not right.

She had to go look for them. As she was moving away from the window, she caught a glimpse of one of the Soar Company employees—his name must have been Sam—looking about him suspiciously, his tall, bulky form clad in a form-fitting black T-shirt and black pants as he approached her room entrance, looking behind one more time.

Immediately, her sixth sense was alert. He scanned the area and pushed through the front door without knocking. She was sure about one thing—Sam was not a friend; he was the enemy. She had to compose herself or else ...

"Mrs. Odhiambo, are you in?" he called, opening the bedroom door.

Gera was behind it and had to hold her breath to prevent him from spotting her. He walked stealthily into the room, searched under the bed, in the closet, and went to the bathroom. She saw it as her only chance to run away.

She tiptoed out of the bedroom and ran for the door. He was very alert and heard her all the same, hot on her heels now. It seemed she was not fast enough, or he was too fast—he was right behind her. He pulled her by her hair, and she cried out in pain.

She had to get away from him.

She tried to pull away, but he held her tightly, and she was not strong enough to evade. She bit his hand, and he groaned in pain. He punched her hard on the left cheek, and she landed on the ground. *The man has a metal fist.* She felt the pain right at the core of her being.

She sat on the ground and could not move, or so he thought. He went to pull her up on her feet. Gera grasped the opportunity and sprayed him in the eye with her olive hair spray which was lying around. He became temporarily blinded, and she got to her feet and ran away.

She rushed outside and did not even know where to run to. She did not want be caught again. Her mind was racing, her heart beating fast. She chose the right turn, away from the beach. She could not see any sign of Loiser or Brandon, and she became even more worried. What if they had been killed? What would happen next?

That thought proved very depressing. She had to remain focused and save herself first if she was going to be of any help to them. Maybe Brandon had been right about suggesting that she take Loiser with her to Nairobi.

She saw one of the men going to her hotel room, and she ducked behind some clothes on the hanglines. Gera was determined to find Loiser and Brandon. She had found that place called happiness with them, and it wasn't just going to slip through her fingers. She was going to fight tooth and nail to save them.

***

Brandon opened his eyes to a dark space that only had a single, small hole near the roof to let in light. The light reminded him of the appearance of angels he had read in Sunday school. However, the room was filled with the odour of urine, faeces, and sweat.

He felt a dull ache at the back of his head. He tried to stretch but found his hands and legs tied to a chair. When he tried to pull free, the rope dug into his skin. He tried even harder and cried out in pain when the rope sliced into his flesh and warm blood inched down his fingers. The blood landed on the cemented floor like raindrops, loud to his ears. He stopped with the ropes and sat upright on his cold, metallic chair.

It took him some minutes to recollect what had led him to this situation. Damn Ken! He was going to kill that son of a gun. He remembered going to find out about Loiser when he was approached by a masked man. He'd tried to fight, but three more men had appeared, forming a ring around him. He'd tried to fight them through kicks and punches, but he had been outnumbered. They'd kicked him, punched him until everything had turned black. He'd felt himself free-falling into a dark pit as he'd tried to hang onto consciousness, but the beatings would not allow him to.

"Hello, Brandon," Ken called from some corner in the room.

Talk of the devil. Brandon's eyes adjusted to the poor lighting, and he saw Ken's blurred frame seated across from him.

"Where are Gera and Loiser, you filthy brute?" he asked, hating the very sight of Ken.

Ken moved closer and dealt him a hefty blow on the nose, another one on the chest, and a heavy kick on the stomach. Brandon went down with the chair, its sharp edges tearing his shoulder like paper. His nose was bleeding. Ken then went and pulled him up with his chair.

"Next time, mind your language. I greeted you. You should have answered. We will start again. Hello, Brandon," Ken went on.

Brandon eyed him deviously. If looks could kill, then Ken would have died right then.

Ken bent to look at him in the eyes, a satisfied grin on his face. It reminded Brandon of a cat who had managed to steal his master's milk. Brandon spat at him. Ken's eyes glittered murderously as he wiped the saliva from his face with a grey handkerchief.

Ken gave him a painful blow to the left eye, and Brandon groaned in pain. His body was vibrating with pain all over. Ken moved back to his seat, watching him intently, a smug smile on his face.

Brandon was bleeding, his clothes drenched in blood and sweat.

When Ken had finished, he moved his seat closer to that of Brandon.

"Let us have a man to man talk now. Seems like we will skip the greeting part," Ken snarled.

Brandon just looked at him, wondering what could make a man so bitter, but he could not come up with even one simple answer.

"You know at the end of this day, you will be no more. Gera and Loiser will also suffer the same fate. You understand what I am saying?" Ken asked him, smirking at the dark look that suddenly clouded his face. "I get it. You understand me. You know, I could even keep Gera after I have killed you. It is just that she is not exactly my type, too feisty for my liking. Your Loiser is also a spoilt brat who will only bring me more headaches, and the perfect plan is to do away with all of you. A clean sweep, leaving no one standing."

Ken gave a loud laugh at his masterpiece plan.

"Why are you doing this, Ken? Can't you just let us live our lives in peace?"

Ken smiled sardonically. "I want to make you see what it means to lose everything. You know, you think life is always easy and simple. Live and let live. Well, sorry to disappoint you, I do not share the same view."

Brandon could not believe that his life was going to end just like this. Yesterday, he seemed to have everything, the love of Gera and his sweet daughter,

Loiser. Today, he was going to lose them and his life, too.

This was not happening. He was not going down without a fight. He'd better die trying than just die.

"I always admired you when we were friends. You were always smart. You had straight As. You seemed to have a way with the ladies. You had everything going for you," he commented. That wasn't true at all, but maybe Ken would be deluded enough to think he meant it.

"Until you took Jackie from me!" Ken barked out.

"What?" Brandon asked, surprised. "I didn't know you also had an interest in Jackie, I swear. I just met her, and we fell in love. You even congratulated us when we told you about our proposed marriage."

"How could you know? You were always full of yourself. Always looking out for your best interest, not caring what I felt. You got married, had a child, a well-paying job, big house, and three cars. You had everything I ever dreamt of as a small boy. I took Jackie from you, but you seemed to move on pretty well. That is why I wanted you to feel it all. How it feels to think you have everything, and then just losing it in a flash," Ken said, small beads of sweat forming on his forehead. "You should know some things about me that you have never bothered to find out, a tour through my life. Sit back and enjoy."

Brandon raised his eyebrows in surprise. He then realized that he knew little about Ken because he rarely talked about his past.

"You know, as a child, I wanted to be loved just like any boy of my age, but nobody was around to do that. My mother was dead, and my dad was too preoccupied with the whores and beer to care. I had to raise myself up. I watched my father every night making out with the whores. I was inquisitive and tried it out on my deskmate, and unfortunately, she got pregnant. The night my father discovered that, he raped me," Ken said, and paused for a while to ensure Brandon was absorbing everything he was saying.

Brandon felt himself turn pale. He had never expected such a grosteque scene to be part of Ken's life. He had maybe seen one in the movies, heard them happening to strangers. He was so mad at Ken's father for making him go through all that. No child was supposed to go through half of what Ken was saying.

"I was so mad at my father, but not for raping me, because thanks to him, I am gay. I really love my life as gay. You may ask yourself then why did I take Jackie from you? Just to spite you. Women don't interest me that much. My father infected me with HIV/AIDS, and now, I have to take drugs for the rest of my life. My life was not as rosy as yours. He died when I was in class seven. It was then that I was taken in by a well-wisher, and life changed for the better.

"But you know, the ghosts from my past kept haunting my life. The good life path is not for me. I have chosen a different path. Hurting people brings me so much pleasure, you can't imagine," he concluded, and an enigmatic light clouded his eyes.

Just then, Brandon saw him for what he was. Ken was a monster. His insides shuddered in fear because he knew Ken was not kidding. He was surely going to wipe out Brandon together with everything that mattered most in his life: Gera and Loiser.

"Okay," he said. "Then, if you are going to kill me, do it like a man. Let us fight this war of death and get it all over with."

Ken laughed mockingly. "Are you kidding me? You think I'll give you the chance to mock me again? No, Brandon, I will not give you that satisfaction of bailing yourself out, because if I die, you remain and emerge the winner. I will not allow you to do that to me. No, Brandon, not again."

"I did not know you could be less masculine. I always thought you were the macho man. Are you going to kill me while tied to a chair? That is not what I call victory. Anyway, get it over with. I want to meet my Creator already," Brandon told him.

He knew he was asking for a bargain with the devil himself, but he did not care. He was desperate and clinging on any straw he could find.

"Boss, what do we do with him?" Philip asked, entering the dark hole. He was carrying a thick piece of metal, his waist adorned by a game knife, which Brandon suspected was very sharp.

"Finish him off, and make sure you bring me the head," Ken ordered as he sauntered out of the dark hole.

And now, fear was indeed crawling through him. Brandon called him, pleading him to spare his family, but he didn't look behind.

"Philip, please listen to me. I thought you were my friend. Don't do this."

"I have a job to do, and it doesn't include making friends," Philip said, raising his rod, which then landed heavily on Brandon's shoulder.

"Arrgh!" he groaned.

He heard his shoulder crack. Pain travelled from the spot, spreading to his whole body.

Chapter Fourteen

Jackie saw Ken leaving and knew the coast was clear. She waited for about ten minutes then leaped out of her hiding place. She tiptoed until she came to the entrance of the dark hole, peeped in but could not see anything because it was pitch black inside. She was still straining to see inside that she did not even notice somebody coming behind her. She only felt a cold metal on her neck and knew she was in trouble.

"Hello, Jackie. Raise your hands," Ken greeted her before she had even turned to look at him.

She slowly turned with her hands in the air.

"Hello, my beloved husband," she said between clenched teeth.

Her plan to save Brandon was not going to be realized. What a pity!

"I cannot believe that you came to save him. You still love him that much?"

"Because you are not a lovable person, Ken, and you will never know what love means," she said defiantly.

When she saw fire flickering in Ken's eyes, she knew she had touched a cord.

"You think that by killing Brandon and his family, you will be happy? Ken, that is not how you find happiness. You cannot be happy by stepping on others and making them suffer. If you are not happy, you cannot make anybody happy because you can't give what you don't have," she told him, hoping he would listen.

What she had not realized was that, for Ken, making people suffer was his haven called happiness. He was happier when others suffered, and especially if that pain was inflicted by him.

"You cannot vouch for him. It is too late for that, Jackie. I think you should go together with him to Hell, you lying, conniving woman," he said with finality.

If Jackie was lying and conniving as he claimed, then *he* had turned her into that, slowly but surely.

He raised his gun to pull the trigger, but she was too fast. She kicked the gun out of his hand before he could shoot, and he was temporarily thrown off balance.

She took out her knife and sliced his leg so deep that blood gushed out like a fountain. She then kicked him severally on the chest, stomach, groin until he went down.

"I love seeing you so powerless, Ken," she said, and he eyed her dangerously. She remembered all the torture he had put her and her son through, and she got even angrier.

She resumed kicking him, until somebody shouted from a distance, "Stop! You are going to kill the bastard."

She stopped abruptly, realizing that Ken had passed out. The police came crowding the area and pulled her away from his bleeding form. They then handcuffed him and lifted him to the waiting police car.

He stirred awake, and Jackie looked him in the eyes. "I hope you find salvation and redemption, Ken. You are going to rot in jail."

She then rushed inside the dark hole to find Brandon lying in pool of blood. She met Philip in handcuffs, being led out by the police. She raised her hand to slap him, but the police stopped her.

She went to Brandon and held him close to her heart. It really felt good to hold him again.

***

Gera roamed the beach, searching for Loiser and Brandon in vain. His colleagues and their families were nowhere to be seen. The afternoon sun had her wiping sweat on her face and her clothes sticking to her body. She sat down on the white sand, dejected.

She was calculating her next move when she heard the siren of a police car. She walked toward the sound and stood at a safe distance, observing everything. An abandoned old building stood out like a sore thumb, and in front of it was a police car and three police officers in uniform. Ken was dragged into the police car in handcuffs.

What was Ken doing here? She watched as the vehicle sped away. Her stomach rumbled loudly with anxiety. She rushed towards the house, hoping that Loiser and Brandon were alive.

She was at the door when she saw Loiser and this strange woman embracing bloody Brandon. She stood rooted to the ground, her heartbeat slowing. She felt dizzy and had to lean on the rusty doorpost. The woman turned her face towards the door, and their eyes met. Her heartbeat picked up speed when she realized it was Jackie, who looked at her smugly and kissed Brandon on the lips. Gera's heart fell to her stomach.

Brandon opened his eyes a fraction, staring straight at her. He stretched his blood-red right hand, but it was limp and fell to his side.

The siren of the ambulance filled the air. Gera walked away from the door to the beach absentmindedly. She felt so cold all of a sudden and so alone in the world.

What had she expected? She did not belong to Brandon. He did not belong to her. She could not blame Loiser, either. The poor kid needed both her parents so much.

She walked away, not looking back. Maybe this was destiny. She felt like crying, but she was not going to be weak.

***

"Clinton, will you come and get me?" she spoke into the phone.

"Gera, are you alright? I'm coming for you right now," he responded after she had told him her location.

Within a short while, his car halted a few meters from the concrete bench where she was seated. It was eight at night, and she was shivering from the cold. Her dress was torn everywhere, her bloody face covered with bruises, her hair a mess.

Clinton went to her on the bench and tightly hugged her.

"Let's go, sweetie," he whispered in her ear.

He led her to the car and drove home. It took about twenty minutes to arrive at his place in Bamburi Estate. All through the journey, silence enveloped the car. When the vehicle halted, he went to open her door, and she got out. They went to his house hand in hand. Clinton unlocked the door and welcomed her into the sitting room.

The room was warm, the walls covered in cream paint. He had brown set of seats which gave the room even more warmth. There was also a very exquisite glass coffee table in the middle of the room. Gera took the love seat and heaved a sigh of relief. Clinton went to the fridge to bring her a jug of mango juice, and she was grateful. He then sat next to her.

"Gera, what happened to you?" He went straight to the core of the matter.

She looked at him straight for the first time, and she liked what she saw. Clinton had grown to be a tall, brown, handsome man. She particularly liked his lips, which she had fallen in love with since their childhood days. He had bedroom eyes which probably drove many women crazy. But tonight, she was not interested in being driven crazy.

"Nothing much," she said after realising that she had been quiet for a while.

"Come on, sweetie. You didn't sound fine when you called me," he urged, taking her hands into his.

Gera felt warm. She realized she did not feel like talking; she just wanted to be taken care of.

"Will you hug me, please?" she asked, and he did just that.

He rubbed his hand all over her back soothingly, and she felt cared for. She and Clinton had made a pact while in the orphanage that should either of them be in trouble, they would call each other. That was exactly what she had done. Tonight, of all the nights, she needed some good, good loving, and she had thought of Clinton first. He had promised to visit after leaving the orphanage, but as years had gone by, she had seen less and less of him until he stopped coming.

She didn't blame him. Life always had a way of getting in between even the strongest relationships. But she'd always had his number, thus able to reach him anytime.

The hug became more than just a hug, the caresses more intense. That's when he kissed her. Her childhood sweetheart, the Clinton she had cherished with the whole of her heart. They explored each other's mouth, searching for that spark that makes a kiss memorable.

But she could not quite locate the spark tonight. Clinton was not Brandon. Only her Brandon could make her come alive. She suddenly broke the kiss, and Clinton did not pursue it further. She started crying out her poor heart, and he held her until she stopped.

"I loved this man very much, and I thought he loved me back. But today, I am not sure. His wife returned, and I think they are back together, and me, on the other hand, is left all alone, Clinton," she told him, still sobbing.

He looked at her understandingly and wiped away her tears. "What makes you think they are back together?"

She recounted the day's ordeal. He nodded while listening to everything she said.

"I'm not defending him, but I think you jumped to conclusions. You did not even accompany them to the hospital to check on his progress. Are you that uncaring, sweetie?"

"But they seemed like they belonged together, and I did not want to intrude. Maybe I ran away because I care about him too much. Do you understand?"

He just looked at her affectionately. "I still think you should go back and check on him like the good girl Mama Jane raised you to be."

Gera sighed. "I will think about it, but I cannot promise you that I will go."

"It's alright, whatever you'll decide. You are still my honey. Cheer up, and let us go cook supper," he told her, getting up and pulling her with him.

Gera was glad she had called him.

Clinton offered to cook them supper, saying he was doing it because she was a visitor. He made rice and beef.

"Gera, how did you become so beautiful over the years?" he asked her.

She blushed and mumbled a reply.

He laughed. "You still blush. I missed you. I think we have been seeing less of each other than we should. I want us to be close friends."

"That would be great, Clinton. I think I will be coming to the coast more frequently for holidays. It is a very interesting place to spend time. The beach, the breeze, the ocean, it is just fantastic," she said with dreamy eyes.

"Now I remember. You always wanted to live on the beach so that you would watch the ocean, the sunrise and sunset," he told her.

Her eyes welled up with tears. She could not believe that he still remembered that.

"Yes, Gera, I remember every moment we spent together. I even wondered sometimes whether we were meant to end up together, after all," he said meaningfully.

She just looked at him, surprised. Years back, she had dreamt of hearing him saying those words, but they never came. Now that she had tangled up with Brandon, she was not sure whether she wanted to hear those words from Clinton. Wrong timing, that's all, she told herself.

"Gera, we still have got a lot of time. You don't have to tell me everything tonight. I will wait."

They ate their supper while chatting about their childhood days in the orphanage and laughing heartily. At about eleven o'clock, they retired to bed, and she took the guest room. The bed was big and welcomed her to sleep, where she forgot everything. She covered herself with a blanket and felt quite warm.

However, sleep was not forthcoming. Over the past few days, she had been accustomed to sleeping with Brandon. Tonight, she felt odd sleeping alone, and she thought of their last encounter. How they had kissed, held each other, and made love.

How could something that felt that good turn out wrong?

Sleep finally came and took her off her depressing thoughts.

***

Gera woke up the next morning to find that she was alone in the house. She walked to the kitchen in

Clinton's oversized shirt. He had left her a note saying that he had gone to work, but she was free to stay for as long as she wanted. She was grateful for his help during her time of need.

She bathed in his big bathroom and wore the knee-length, green dress which he had bought for her. She then had breakfast, pondering whether to go to the hospital or not. She was still raking up her brain when her phone rang. Brandon's name lit the screen. She picked up the phone happily.

The smile died on her lips when she heard a woman's voice.

"Stay away from us, you whore. You should know your place. We don't need you in our lives!"

She knew immediately that it just had to be Jackie. Her heart shattered into a million pieces. Maybe going to the hospital was not a good idea, after all. She could not stay at Clinton's place for long. She just wanted to go back to Kisumu.

Chapter Fifteen

Gera boarded the Mash Poa Coach to Kisumu. She slept throughout the journey to escape her thoughts, wanting to block everything from her mind. During the trip, she had dreams. She dreamt that she was in Brandon's house. She was his wife, and Loiser was playing in the backyard. She was cooking lunch, and Brandon came and held her from behind. She felt so loved.

She opened her eyes twelve hours later only to find that they were already in Kisumu. She took a *bodaboda* from Kisumu Stage to Brandon's home in Mamboleo. The watchman allowed her in, and she took all her belongings, which were just two bags stuffed with clothes and shoes.

She walked from room to room, allowing the memories to wash through her. Every room held memories, special ones close to her heart. She walked out of the house, giving it one last look. This had been her home for the last year. Now, she had none. Maybe she was always meant to be alone and unhappy. Happiness was just out of her reach.

She took another motorbike to Action Hotel in Kondele where she was going to put up for the night. When she reached the hotel, she quickly bathed and retired to bed. She had to start thinking about her future. She had some money in the bank. They could push her for six months only. After that, she did not know.

Maybe she was going to start drawing seriously and sell her drawings. Not a bad idea, she thought as she drifted off to sleep.

***

Brandon woke up at the Aga Khan Hospital feeling so groggy and in pain everywhere. He expected to find Gera by his bedside, but he was very disappointed when he saw Jackie instead sitting and waiting patiently next to him. He then remembered Gera's departure and understood everything. So Gera had thought they were back together with Jackie? His poor Gera, he thought.

Brandon knew that right now, she was hurting and really needed him. Gera was dead wrong. There was no way he was going back with Jackie. He could not even imagine doing that in his wildest dreams. Right now, he really wanted to be with Gera.

Jackie stood up from the chair to embrace him, but the look that met her stopped her in her tracks.

"What's wrong, Brandon? What have I done for you to be this cold towards me?" she asked, her voice trembling with emotions.

He just chuckled. "You have done nothing, Jackie. But maybe it's high time you did something. Leave me in peace. I don't want to ever see you again!"

Sadness clouded her eyes, but that didn't move him.

"Brandon, I am not leaving again. Not this time. For the first time, I am going to fight for what I want, and that is to be with you and Loiser," she said, looking at him.

"You should have thought of that before you left. Now it's a little too late, don't you think?" he said sarcastically.

This argument with Jackie was weighing him down. Everything had happened in the past, and there was no use reliving it. He just wanted her to go west while he went east. For them, the past could not just be reconciled with the present. It was a lost cause.

Jackie's face contorted with so much sadness, and she began crying. He was not always comfortable with seeing a woman's tears, but he was not moved by hers. Even the softest of hearts could be hardened. Jackie was conniving, and he no longer knew what to believe or not to believe. Maybe the tears were just crocodile tears she was using to get to him.

The doctor entered the room and found Jackie wailing uncontrollably on the floor. She was tearing at her clothes and throwing her hands in the air. They asked her to leave because she was stressing the patient.

Brandon felt guilty for not caring about her, but he could not help it. He had chosen to tightly lock her far away, but she was forcing that door open and making him feel the pain all over again. He had given her everything that a woman could ever dream of, but she had thrown that to the wind and followed Ken. That was equal to mocking his ego, an unforgivable sin.

***

The doctors took Jackie outside and told her to give the patient some time to recover before they could solve their 'issues.' Jackie was desperate. She was hanging by a rope and didn't just know what to do anymore with her life.

She was thirty-two years old and had a son. Double tragedy. Most of the men of her age were already married. Who was going to marry her? Ken was definitely going for life sentence, not that she was even considering going back with him. Brandon just had to accept her back whether he liked it or not.

She had resigned from her job a year ago just to please Ken. She did not even know where to start looking for one. Her life was a mess. Only God knew when this nightmare was going to end. Maybe it was high time she went back to her native home. But most of her agemates were happily married while she was an unmarried woman with a son. She was going to be the talk of the village.

That was not something she was ready for. Maybe when worse came to worst, she would consider that possibility. For the moment, she was going to play her cards well and ensure she won back Brandon. Even if it meant blackmail and manipulation, she was ready.

***

"Daddy, wake up," Loiser called.

Brandon opened his eyes and was immensely happy to see her daughter. Only yesterday, he had been on the verge of losing her. He hugged her affectionately. Ken had lost once more. Or maybe he had won on one account—taking Gera away from him. But Brandon had to be grateful that Gera was alive. Once he was back on his feet, he swore to look for her everywhere and convince her to go back to him.

Loiser slowly pulled away from him. "Where is Gera?"

He had been dreading that question because he didn't know the answer to it. The look of hope on Loiser's face told him she was hoping to hear some good news. She was still young, and she had a lot of things to learn about life. One lesson was that you cannot always have what you want in life. Sometimes, you succeed, and at times, you fail, and that was the beauty of life.

"I don't know, Loiser. I have not seen her since yesterday. But don't worry, she will come back," he explained, and she looked at him suspiciously, like she suspected her father was hiding something from her.

"When is she coming back?" she asked stubbornly.

"Tell the poor thing the truth, please!" Jackie impatiently said, entering the room.

Brandon eyed her deviously and said nothing. Loiser looked from him to Jackie.

"The so-called Gera is not coming back here, Loiser. I will take care of you from now onwards," Jackie said, smiling sweetly at her.

Loiser didn't react. She just stood there unsmiling, crossing her arms on her petite chest.

"Daddy, please tell me that it's not true. I want Gera," she said, looking at her father.

Brandon was at a crossroad. He called Loiser and hugged her, then asked her to leave him alone with Jackie. Loiser left the room without a second glance at her mother.

"What are you trying to do, Jackie? And why are you so sure that Gera isn't coming back?" he asked, disgusted by the very sight of her.

"I called her and told her not to bother us again. Is there something wrong with that? I understand she was just your househelp, and since I'm back, we don't need her services," Jackie explained.

Brandon didn't know whether to be mad or laugh.

"Jackie! Jackie. There is no us; there will never be. I don't even know who gave you the right to go snooping around my phone and calling Gera. You have wrecked enough havoc in our lives. Aren't you tired?" he told her harshly, his eyes stone-cold.

Jackie walked out of the room smiling and swinging her hips. Brandon shook his head in disbelief.

***

Gera went house-hunting with Rosie the next day. They had connected again. Rosie was very sorry for her, but she told her that everything was going to work out fine. They found a bedsitter in Migosi Estate. The house was superb. It had white walls, light blue tiles on the floor, and the neighbourhood was safe. The house felt like home. It felt more like Brandon's home because Brandon's home was the only place she had found happiness. She was going to make her home a happy haven.

"Your sister, Queen, is going to have a baby," Rosie said, startling Gera so much that she stopped midway her tour.

"What do you mean, Rosie?" she asked, fearing the answer already.

She had chosen to let the past rest and had not even contacted Queen and her mother to find out how they were faring. It was after leaving Brandon's house that she'd felt the past weighing heavily on her. Of late, she was realizing that no matter how fast she was running away from the past, it was slowly catching up with her.

"Queen is pregnant, and the father of the baby is not willing to take responsibility. She is now staying with your mother in Oyugis Town. They are very miserable, Gera. You should pay them a visit," Rosie pleaded.

Gera remembered how her mother had abandoned her and Queen at the orphanage. She felt so much heaviness in her heart. She just couldn't let the matter rest. Queen had been very young and she could not vividly remember what had happened, and maybe that was why she had been very forgiving.

"I met Queen at the market last month. She was very thin, her eyes sunken and sad. They are staying in a small one-roomed mabati house at the market center. They barely have enough to eat, and Queen is working as a househelp for Mama Onyango where she is being paid one hundred shillings per day. Your mother is also ailing."

Her stomach turned upon hearing this. But still, should she go see them, after everything?

***

Brandon could not stand it anymore. He really wanted to see Gera. It was now becoming a necessity—more like the air he breathed. He had called her severally, but she was not picking his calls. He had even sent her a message hoping that she would reply, but he should have known better.

They had flown back to Kisumu after three days, and the doctor had recommended f lots of bed rest. He was feeling much better, though. The painkillers the doctors had prescribed for him were working miracles. Jackie had tagged along, bringing her son with her.

He was tired of arguing with her. It seemed that her mind was set on staying, so he let her. But one thing was for sure—he was going to treat her like she was invisible. There was no way they were going back to the era before the Ken incident. Jackie had to be kidding herself.

"I have brought you mango juice, darling," she said sweetly, putting the tray on the bedside stool.

He was grateful for all her effort. She had been taking good care of him ever since she'd come back. The problem was that he no longer trusted her.

He drank the mango juice cautiously. He wasn't sure what bag of tricks she had up her sleeve. He feared that Jackie might even drug him.

"Come on, Brandon. I might be a lot of things, but I am not a murderer. If I was to do that, you'll be six feet under. Relax your guard," she said jokingly.

Sometimes, women could be so cunning. He was afraid that she might even go to *Dumba wa Dumbwa* to get love potions in order to trap him. He could not just see himself spending the rest of his life with her because that was going to be pure torture.

"I will try to do that. Where is Loiser?" he asked, because he had not seen her since their return from Mombasa.

"I haven't seen her all morning. It's high time she behaves or else ..." She left the statement hanging and went to wake up Loiser, only to return shortly after. "Your daughter is nowhere to be seen. Do you happen to have any clues about where she could have headed?"

After raking his brain for a while, he had an idea where Loiser might have gone, but he didn't just want to believe it. He was suspecting that she might have gone to look for Gera. He was almost sure of it, because where else could she have gone?

The only problem he was facing was that Gera wasn't picking up his calls, and Loiser wasn't picking hers, too, and that made it even more difficult to know where to start looking. He had to do something, all the same.

***

Gera was doing a portrait of one of Rosie's friends when her phone rang. The screen displayed that it was Loiser. She ignored the first call. When the phone started ringing again, she picked it up, worried that maybe Loiser was in trouble.

"Hello?"

"Hello! Gera, where are you?" Loiser asked urgently.

"Loiser, are you alright?"

"No. I am not. I want to see you, please," she pleaded, her voice almost cracking because of tears.

"You know where Migosi Estate is?"

"Yes, I do. I will be there in ten minutes."

"I will be waiting for you," she said, then hung up the phone.

After twenty minutes, Loiser alighted from a *matatu*. From her shabby appearance, Gera suspected that she had left in a hurry. Loiser was so happy to see her that she ran to her and embraced her tightly, almost knocking her down. Gera held her close, her heart welling up with so much joy. She had thought she would never set eyes on Loiser again, but here she was.

Loiser looked so tired, and the bags beneath her eyes proved that she had not been getting enough sleep. Gera just wondered silently what was wrong as they went hand in hand to her house. Loiser surveyed the interior while she went to prepare her tea.

"So tell me, how have you been faring on, Loiser? I really missed you," she said, caressing Loiser's back as she took her tea.

"You are lying to me. You went away without telling me," Loiser mumbled.

Gera just smiled sweetly at her. It had been a hard decision to make, but it had to be made.

"Please forgive me, Loiser. I should have said something, but I didn't know whether you would have understood," she explained.

Loiser just shrugged it off as she continued sipping her tea.

"Let's go back home, Gera. My father and I want you back. Promise me we will go back," she said, looking at her hopefully.

Gera did not want to disappoint her, but she could not help it.

"I wish I could come back, but that's just not possible. Now you know where to get me if you want to speak to me, right?" she convinced her.

"But it won't be the same," Loiser complained further.

"I know. I miss you, too," Gera said, and Loiser, seeming to see no light at the end of the tunnel, let the matter rest.

"I wish I could stay here with you forever. Mum and Dad are always quarrelling."

"Sorry about that. I hope things will be fine with time, you will see."

"Maybe. I don't know."

They talked for hours as they lay on the bed, and Gera was grateful for the distraction. Loiser became her old self again, chatting away as if she had swallowed a radio.

The sky outside was darkening.

"Young lady, let me take you home. I know your father is worried sick about you."

Loiser grumpled and mumbled as she faced the wall. "I don't want to go, Gera. I tell you, my house is a boxing ring. I always lock myself in my room."

Before Gera could ask more questions, her phone rang. It was Brandon calling her. She had been avoiding his calls, but at this moment, she suspected he was calling about Loiser. He must have been very worried about her. She received the call—this was not about them.

"Finally, you have decided to pick my calls. Is Loiser with you?" he asked.

"Yes, Brandon," she answered him tersely.

She was not going to show him just how much hearing his voice again had affected her. She was going to act like it was normal and it didn't matter a bit.

"Alright, give me your location so that I can come for her," he said to her.

Loiser looked dejected for a while before mumbling that she would come and visit Gera whenever she had the chance.

Soon after, Brandon halted his car at Gera's front door and alighted. She was already waiting for him by the door. One quick sweep of her with his eyes, and he smiled as if pleased.

He walked to her in three long strides. She had been nervous about meeting him again, not knowing what to expect. She still held feelings for him in her heart. Too bad Fate was not on her side. She wondered why life was sometimes unfair. All she had ever wanted was to be with Brandon, but even that chance, she had been denied.

"Aren't you letting me in, Gera? Or do I have to use force to get into your house?" he inquired when he saw how reluctant she was to move from the door.

"Good evening, Brandon. Where are your manners? Didn't your mother teach you that you should greet people when you meet them?" she teased him.

"She did. In fact, she told me to do this," he said, moving closer and suprising her with a kiss on the lips.

She wanted to push him away, but she couldn't get the strength or the mind to do so.

She pulled away just an inch to look into his eyes. "Then you are even more mannerless than I thought."

He chuckled, looking into her eyes, searching.

"Loiser!" she called out.

She could not allow Brandon into her house. She didn't want to be haunted for the days to come. He was surely going to leave the house smelling of him, feeling of him, and full of him, and then she would visualize him sitting on the bed like he would have done. She couldn't take that. She wanted to create different memories for her house. It was clear enough that Brandon wasn't meant for her, and therefore, she didn't want to build false hopes.

"There you are," he said when finally, Loiser came out. "Goodbye, Gera, and thank you for keeping Loiser safe with you," he added, smiling, but there was a pained look in his eyes.

She just nodded because she didn't trust her voice to be steady. Loiser hugged her and strolled to the car to wait for her father.

Gera watched as he walked away to his car and felt tears coming to her eyes. It had been easier living without them these past few days. She had even started to convince herself that she was better off without them. Seeing them only made her realize how lonely and empty her life was.

Brandon turned to look at her before climbing to the driver's seat and waved. She waved back.

She got inside the house after they drove away, went to her bed, and cried. She cried for a long time until her eyes turned red and puffy. She tightly held her big white teddy bear and slept. She didn't want to think of Brandon and Loiser because she was only going to cry some more.

***

Gera had been in a short, sleeveless red dress that clung to her figure like polythene. The song that had come to his head was 'Lady in Red.' And he wondered if she had dressed like that intentionally to tip him off balance.

Brandon had thought she was bluffing about not letting him in. When she had called Loiser out, he'd realized that she had been serious. He couldn't blame her. She had her reasons for doing that. Loiser had taken her time, probably to give them a chance to talk. She had looked much better than she had been some days back. Gera had cheered her up, and for that, he was going to be forever grateful.

He hadn't wanted to leave. His place was beside Gera. He felt alive and vibrant with her. He had hesitated in leaving, but had finally walked away to his car. If he would have stayed much longer, he suspected he might have changed his mind altogether and not left.

He was worried about her, though. She was out here all alone. What if something bad happened to her?

It was too late to think of that. Gera was a fully grown woman, and she could take care of herself.

With that conviction in his mind, he drove away. He was going to come back maybe after two days to check if she was doing alright, but he knew he was kidding himself. He would be coming back for more than one reason.

He drove to Mamboleo while his head and heart remained at Migosi. He was forever going to love Gera. Jackie was never going to replace Gera no matter what she did. Gera was sweet, loving, and caring. She knew how to pull his heart strings like no other. By just seeing her, health-wise, he felt better already.

Gera knew how to live life to the fullest and bring out the best in him. Jackie, on the other hand, was doing the complete opposite these days.

Chapter Sixteen

One month passed, and things were looking up for Gera. Her drawing business was picking up, and she had lots of orders, so much so that she barely had time to do anything else. She was very good at what she did, and within no time, word about her expertise had spread like bush fire. She was busy every day doing portraits, and she was very proud of herself. She only had one problem—or was it a blessing in disguise? After a month of her departure from Mombasa, she had started having morning sickness.

The doctor confirmed her fear that she was actually pregnant. At first, she had been depressed, about bringing up a fatherless child. But she'd then refused to be put down by the thought. She was going to bring up her child with all the love she held in her heart.

At least, she was going to have a reminder of Brandon and the time they'd shared. She loved the baby already. She sat everyday on the rocking chair talking to it. She was not sure whether she wanted a girl or a boy. Nonetheless, she didn't care because she just felt so much love for her child.

***

It was early in the morning, and the sun was slowly rising from the horizon, warming the earth's surface.

Brandon was sitting on his rocking chair, basking in the glow. He was still in his blue bathrobe, and today, he just felt that he had to see Gera again. Ever since that day he'd seen her in Migosi, he hadn't set his eyes on her again. He missed her terribly.

Making love with Jackie was even unthinkable. He could not even imagine touching her, let alone making love to her. It wasn't that Jackie had not tried various tricks to arouse him. But every time she did, he was so repulsed that he felt shivers inching down his body. If they were going to stay together, it was out of being grateful for saving him from Ken as she claimed, not love. Brandon could not even start to imagine how boring and dim his life was going to get if he got back with her permanently.

***

Her baby bump had started to show, and Gera now wore free dresses which were very beautiful. Like the one she was wearing today was black and lacy. She looked at herself in the mirror, caressing her stomach, and thought she looked more beautiful than ever. Maybe she was going to have a baby girl. She was getting more and more tired these days, but she had a housegirl who came to do housework during the day. She now had more time to rest and draw.

She heard a rap on the door and went to open, expecting her housegirl, but instead, she found Jackie standing there.

"What do you want? How did you know where I live?" Gera asked rudely and did not care.

Jackie just smiled at her. "Can't you invite me in first before asking me a thousand and one questions?"

Jackie then pushed her aside forcefully and barged into the house. Gera got angry, and the baby kicked her stomach quite hard and she winced in pain. The baby did not like her getting angry. She locked the door behind her and walked back to the room where she found Jackie admiring her portraits.

"You know, you are no longer in my house, but Brandon and Loiser still walk around the place longing for you. It really pains me to know that," Jackie concluded, taking one of the seats.

Jackie was in black jeans and a very expensive red top that reminded Gera of how different their economic statuses were. For a moment, she wondered why she had to appear in her house unannounced. She had everything that Gera had ever dreamed of, yet here she was.

"Well, thanks. I did not know," she said, looking at Jackie. She wondered whether this was the only thing that had brought the woman to her house.

"This is all a big joke to you, isn't it?" Jackie asked angrily, getting up from her seat like it had suddenly become too hot.

She charged toward her, and Gera put her hands over her stomach, protecting her baby. She landed on her chair with a thud, felt an excruciating pain in her stomach, and let out a loud cry. As if that was not enough, Jackie started pulling her by the hair.

It was at that moment that Brandon rushed into the room and found Jackie hurting her.

"Stop it, Jackie! What in God's name are you doing?" he shouted.

Jackie abruptly left her hair and straightened up. "I should be asking you the same question. What are you doing in this whore's house?"

"Get out, Jackie!" he barked at her, rushing to Gera.

Jackie knew better than to continue arguing at the dark, hooded look he gave her. She walked out without even uttering a word.

Brandon rushed to embrace Gera. She clung to him, too. She had been so afraid that she was going to lose the baby.

"I am here, love," he whispered in her ear.

Oh, how he smelt so right and felt so good.

At that moment, the baby kicked, and he moved away from her. He hesitantly put his hands on her stomach, and the baby kicked again.

"The baby is greeting its father," she told him.

He looked momentarily puzzled.

"Yes, Brandon, you are going to be a father," she explained tenderly.

***

This was one of the best news he had received in a very long time. He lowered his mouth to hers and claimed it. She tasted so good, and he wondered how he had survived this long without kissing her.

When the kiss was over, they were both in need of something more. Damn! It had been a long time. He carried her to the bed. They were naked in no time. He was very gentle with her because he did not want to hurt the baby. Gera was so receptive, and it took all he had to be tender. When it was all over, they were spent and slept for a while.

She woke up to find him kissing her stomach.

"That is so sweet," she told him, tears welling up her eyes.

"Why didn't you inform me earlier, Gera?" he asked, not very happy about being kept in dark.

"I did not want to disrupt your life. Remember that you are a married man," she said bitterly.

"But you know I still deserved to know, nonetheless," he went on stubbornly.

This time, she did not answer—she just looked at him with a far away look. He dropped the issue and resumed kissing her full on the lips. They made sweet love some more.

His gaze roamed to the wall where he saw a portrait of him hanging. His eyes widened in surprise as he moved closer to it. The picture looked exactly like him; exactly as he had looked that morning when he had glanced into the mirror.

"You like it?" Gera asked.

"No. It is perfect. I love it. When did you do it?"

"While I was still staying with you."

"How come you didn't show it to me?"

"I don't know," she said, shrugging.

"My wicked, secretive woman," he said, pulling her into his arms again.

Gera went into his embrace willingly. He kissed the whole of her body so tenderly, whispering sweet nothings.

***

When they woke up again, it was evening. Brandon put on his clothes and said he was leaving. Gera almost screamed in frustration but held herself before she did.

"I am not your *mpango wa kando*. I don't want to see you again, Brandon. I hope you respect that. I don't go around sleeping with married men. Be man enough to accord me and you some respect," she told him, her eyes brimming with tears.

This was not some candy shop, where he could come and get some candy then leave, she thought. Brandon angrily stormed out of the room. She knew maybe he would never come back, but she wanted all or nothing at all. She didn't want to be his mistress. She wanted a father for her baby and a husband for herself.

Maybe she was asking for too much, but it was what her heart desired. That place called happiness would only be complete if she had Brandon fully, not in part. She was not ready to receive love in small doses. She wanted the full dose or no dose at all.

***

Gera heard a rap at the door and limped to it, pelvic pain making walking difficult. She was due in two days, after all. She smiled widely when she found Clinton at her doorstep. He'd promised to be there for her for the birth, and here he was, dressed in a black T-shirt and a pair of blue jeans.

"Mmm, you look so handsome," she said by way of greeting, and Clinton smiled widely, mumbling, "thanks." He hugged her and walked into the house.

"Welcome. How was your journey?"

"It was short and comfortable. Kenya Airways services are very efficient."

"That's great."

"Pregnancy suits you, Gera."

"Thank you. Although, right now, I feel like a hippo."

Clinton shook his head. "No way!"

The maid offered them mango juice, which they drank while chatting animatedly.

***

It was about one in the morning when an unbelievable pain woke Gera up. She slowly got off the bed and sat up. The television was still on. She managed to walk to the sitting room where Clinton was and called to him. He did not hear because he was sound asleep on the couch. She patted him on the arm, and he woke up with a start.

"Oh, Gera, what is it?"

"I feel the painful contractions. Take me to the hospital, please," she said breathlessly.

He took her hand and slowly led her to the car and drove very quickly to the Aga Khan Hospital. On arrival, the nurses quickly took over, and he waited on the seats outside the ward.

***

Brandon finally made up his mind. He could not lose Gera. He realized that life was too short to spend it being unhappy. He was the happiest man when he was with Gera. Since Jackie had no plans of leaving, he had decided to leave instead.

He was packing his clothes when she walked in.

"Are you going for a trip?"

He just continued with his task, ignoring her.

"You are packing all your clothes?" she observed, rushing into the room.

Silence.

"Come on, Brandon. We were getting along so well. I already apologized. Just tell me what to do to make it up to you, please."

He finished packing his clothes, zipped the suitcase, and directed his attention onto her.

"I think it's high time we parted ways, Jackie. I don't love you like I used to, and I don't think I ever will. There is only one woman for me, and that's Gera," he told her.

She shook her head in disbelief. Tears cascaded down her face, and she went down on her knees to beg him.

"Please, Brandon, don't do this. I promise to never go anywhere near Gera," she pleaded, holding his right leg tightly.

He wasn't hearing any of it. He was fed up with her lies and deception. He had just hit the rock's bottom.

"Jackie, please don't make this harder than it is. You can have the house and everything in it," he said, taking the suitcase.

He was choosing his happiness before everything else. He didn't have time for her melodrama.

He dragged his suitcase out of the room. Even if he stayed to listen to her pleas, there was no way he was going to change his mind. Jackie followed him, wailing. This was too bad as it was. He put his case in the car boot and climbed into the driver's seat.

Jackie stood in front of the car, daring him to run over her. He got out of the car and carried her to the house. She was kicking and biting him, but he had no option. He locked her in there. He then drove very fast, trying to create as much distance between him and his house. He was finally free. The feeling of freedom was so exhilarating and rejuvenating. He was finally going to be in Gera's arms where he belonged.

He showed up at her house at eight in the morning, wanting to tell her the good news. He knocked on the door for a while before it was opened by a strange woman, who informed him that she was Gera's housegirl. She explained to him that Gera was in the hospital, delivering.

The thought almost made his head ache. He quickly went to the hospital, driving at a supersonic speed.

It did not take him long to locate her ward. His excitement made him just enter the room. He found Gera lying on the bed—she had just delivered twins. Rosie was holding one child in her arm, and a man he had never seen was holding the other one.

His enthusiasm faded away. Was she already in love with this man? The thought made him coil with jealousy. When they noticed that he was in the room, a pin-drop silence enveloped the room. Gera then whispered to the man to excuse them.

The guy left the room half-heartedly, dragging Rosie with him, and told Gera, "In case of anything, I'm outside."

To Brandon, he gave a look that spoke of hostility, then brushed past him as he went out of the door.

Brandon and Gera looked at each other for a while. He, at this moment, loved her even more.

"Are you going to stand there all day?" she teased him, and it was all the beckoning he needed to go to her.

He kissed the twins swaddled in blue shawls on the forehead and kissed her full on the lips.

"They are adorable," he said, taking one of the babies. One was a boy, the other a girl. He could look at them all day, and he did not think he'd get bored.

"They are my babies, Brandon," she said defiantly, and he looked up from the babies to her and had to laugh.

"So selfish. They are mine, too. I contributed to them being here, remember," he reminded her.

She just shrugged, as if not convinced. The twins dozed off, and she placed the two of them on the bed to sleep peacefully. Now that only the two of them were here, they remained in an awkward silence.

But not for long.

He removed the velvet maroon ring box from his pocket and opened it, revealing a shiny ring with crystal green stones. "Will you marry me, Geraldine Aketch Okumu?"

***

This was unbelievable! Gera almost screamed "Yes."

She thought at first that she was dreaming and she had to pinch herself, but again, she was not going to give in easily. She knew that men liked to work for what they wanted. Why not make him sweat it a little bit?

"Oh, is that so?" she asked, disinterested.

"Come on, Gera. I want to make you my wife. I cannot live without you," he pleaded.

"If my memory is serving me right, Jackie moved in together with you, right? I cannot play second fiddle, Brandon. It has to be all or nothing," she said, liking the surprised look on his face.

If he thought that she was going to take a back seat, he was dead wrong. She wanted all or nothing. She didn't want love in small doses—she wanted love in full dose.

"Gera, please stop rubbing it in like that. Jackie seemed to stick to me like glue. She did not want to leave, but then, I figured out that I might as well be the one to move out. I have left the house and everything in it for her, Gera. I really want to be with you," he pleaded.

"Then I should be thanking you for making that smart move, Brandon. Congratulations! How can we be sure that she won't come back and take you away again?" she said, staying aloof.

He had finally decided to leave Jackie of his own accord just to be with her. She felt her heart welling up with joy. Just when she had thought that all the hope of being with him was lost, here he was proposing marriage.

"That is up to you, Gera. All you have to do is say yes. I just came to the realization that life without you isn't worth living. I don't want to go through life asking myself, 'What if.' You make me happy, Gera. What is the purpose of life without happiness?" he asked, looking deep into her eyes.

Gera didn't even flinch.

At this, he changed tact. He moved closer to her and kissed her before she could offer any more resistance. They said actions speak louder than words. At first, she was startled, but as he deepened the kiss, she could no longer stay indifferent. She responded with a longing of her own. She let herself go and be engulfed in this force greater than her, greater than him. She was forced to bow to its will.

"I never figured that you could show me better than you could tell me, sweetheart," he said, pulling just an inch away from her.

She looked him in the eye and saw all the love there—her eyes, too, mirroring her feelings. She had tried to deny in her head whether such feelings were possible, but her heart knew better. Whoever sang the song 'The heart is not so smart' couldn't have been farther from the truth.

She held Brandon's face and kissed his forehead, then his eyes, his nose, his cheeks, and then lingered before kissing him on the lips.

He looked deep into her eyes and whispered, "I have missed you so much. I want to you to be mine forever."

"Please, Brandon, do not bluff with a woman about marrying her," she told him.

"I'm very serious, Gera. Please just say yes," he pleaded.

"Yes, Brandon, I will gladly marry you," she said, almost jumping off the bed to embrace him.

He slipped the engagement ring in her finger, and it fitted perfectly.

They sealed the deal with a kiss. Finally, she had all she ever wanted. Gera had really wanted a husband, children, and a home full of love. Brandon, on the other hand, had a daughter and a home. But home was not home until she came as part of the package. Both of them had found that place called happiness in each other.

***

"Where are we going?" Gera asked impatiently as they drove towards town after leaving the hospital.

Brandon kept saying that it was a surprise and he didn't want to spoil it for her. The car finally halted at Milimani Estate, outside a mansion. It was surrounded by a stone wall and the black metallic gate which was decorated with tiny blue flowers all over. He proceeded into the compound, and Gera couldn't believe her eyes. She slowly walked out of the car.

"This is our new home. Do you like it?"

"It's perfect," she said, hugging him, and he swung her round and round, Gera laughing.

He loved the sound of her laughter, and he hoped he would be the kind of husband she always wished for.

Loiser rushed out of the house to greet them. She almost knocked Gera down as she hugged her. "Mama, how are you?"

"I am fine," she answered, her face showing she was still not used to the fact that Loiser insisted on calling her 'mama.'

Loiser went to the backseat and carried one of the twins who was still sleeping. Some of her friends rushed forward to help with the other twin.

Brandon held Gera's hand and led her into the house. She walked through every room and could not hide her delight. The house was fully furnished. The sitting room had a cream L- shaped couch, and the cream, soft carpet caressed her feet. There was a thirty-inch flat screen TV set. The dining room had a round table made of smooth mahogany wood. The chairs were of the same wood but had brown leather cushions. The kitchen was so spacious and had many cupboards. Utensils were already well-arranged in them.

"When did you do all this?" she asked, still looking around.

"I bought the house, and I was lucky that it was fully furnished. Is there anything you would like to change?"

"I haven't come across any. Let's see the bedrooms."

The started with the children's bedroom; there were three. But Gera pointed out loud whether the twins would be using them soon. Loiser's room was painted pink and had a comfy king-size bed and walk-in wardrobe. There were two guest rooms similar to Loiser's. And their bedroom was so spacious and had only the four-poster bed which occupied the middle of the space. There was also a beautiful net which had red frills. The bathroom had a white bathtub. They walked through a connecting door which was the cloak room equipped with walk-in wardrobes and shoe racks.

Gera turned and kissed Brandon so tenderly, caressing his face.

"Thank you," she whispered, tone filled with awe and reverence.

"Come, I want to show you something," he said, taking her hand and leading her to another room that she hadn't even noticed because it was on the far corner.

He opened the door, and the light that streamed in through the big window brightened the space. Gera walked into the spacious room which had only a stool and all the things she needed for her drawings which were on a small table.

She held the pencils in her hand, touching the plain papers in awe. She then turned to him.

"I love you, Brandon Odhiambo," she whispered, hugging him.

"I love you, too. I want to make you the happiest woman on Earth," he said, pulling her even closer to him 'til he felt her heart beating fast.

"I am the happiest woman," she said, looking deep into his eyes.

Brandon knew then that had he not met Gera, his life would not have been complete. He knew for sure that he would have wandered the world in search of her, even if he hadn't known what he was searching for.

***

Gera couldn't shake the feeling that absolute happiness wasn't within her reach. Of course, Brandon was good to her most of the time, ever since she'd moved into their house in Milimani. Loiser was also great. Her twins were growing up fast. She was now drawing full time, yet she still felt empty in some deepest part of her soul, an emptiness that all their love could not fill.

She decided to drive to the orphanage to see Mama Jane. She always had all the answers to her problems. When she alighted from her car, Mama Jane went to embrace her. She opened up the car boot where there were many paper bags of shopping. The older boys and girls scrambled to carry them to the store room.

"Gera, what a nice surprise! You are looking good," Mama Jane said, giving her the once- over.

"Thank you. You have to help me carry one of them," Gera said, handing her one of the twins.

Mama Jane held her close to her bosom, adjusting the shawl. She then led the way to her office.

"You have been gone for so long," she said after taking her seat.

"I know. I am sorry about that. I should have called, but a lot had been going on in my life. I know it all sounds like an excuse."

"Don't beat yourself up too much. I understand how life sometimes gets in the way," Mama Jane said.

Gera filled her in on her marriage to Brandon and how he was a wonderful husband.

"But?" Mama Jane asked.

She had to smile. She had forgotten Mama Jane's ability to read her thoughts. The older woman always seemed to know her better than she knew herself.

"Of late, I have been feeling unhappy. I have everything, but I still feel like I am missing some vital part."

"What do you think brings about the sadness?"

"I don't know."

"Have you ever tried to contact you mother or Queen?"

Gera shook her head, and she saw the disappointment in Mama Jane's eyes.

"Don't get angry at me, please. I have tried, but every time, I face a brick wall," she pleaded, before the twin she was carrying started to cry. She breastfed him as Mama Jane looked at her, marveling at how life changes very fast.

"You have to let go of the past hurt and open up your heart for love and happiness," Mama Jane said, her voice echoing in the room.

Gera shook her head in protest.

"What if I can't let go of the hurt?" she asked, fearing the answer she was going to get.

"Then I'm sorry. Forget about that place called happiness. You can never be truly happy when you still walk around with the past weighing heavily on you. It's like tying a stone to your ankle and still expecting to stay afloat."

Gera left that day, her heart heavier than when she had arrived, but she acknowledged that there was truth and wisdom in all that Mama Jane had said.

Chapter Seventeen

Gera was seated under a coconut tree, feeling the cool December breeze from the Indian Ocean. She was in her very sexy, blue bikini, and she was feeling sweet sixteen. They had decided to go to the coast for their annual vacation. Brandon wasn't for the idea because Mombasa held scary memories for him—memories of Ken, almost losing his life and losing Gera, but she had insisted, and he'd granted her wish.

She looked on as Brandon, her dearest husband, played with their three children. Loiser had insisted on naming the twins Maya and Gaya, and they had let her. The twins were now two years old and very adorable, identical and very naughty. They both wanted to put on dresses. Gera was fine with the arrangement, but her husband wasn't hearing any of it. They were both in blue shorts and white vests. A stranger could not even tell them apart. The twins seemed to love the confusion.

Loiser had grown up to be a beautiful lady. She and Gera were getting along well, more like sisters rather than mother and daughter. Stanley had asked her out tonight, and they were going on their first real date, Stanley and his family vacationing close by. Everything Gera had ever dreamed of had come true; she could not ask for more.

The ball accidentally hit her, and she threw it back to Brandon who then winked at her, and she blushed from head to toe. He smiled knowingly and resumed playing with the impatient children.

Her heart welled with so much love for all of them. She just wondered what had just driven her mother to abandon both Queen and her at the orphanage. All the explanations she gave could not suffice. The only mother, real mother, Gera had known was Mama Jane. Mama Jane had been there for her at every critical point of her life—when she had her menarch, when she got her first boyfriend. Mama Jane had always advised her appropriately.

Her real mother had failed miserably in her duty as a mother. To Gera, her mother was dead. No mother could easily give up her daughters to remarry another man. Maybe one day, she was going to find it in her heart to forgive her. She was just not ready. She was not as easily forgiving as Queen. The Lord knew how hard she had tried but just could not forgive her parent. All those times she'd cried, all alone and in need of love in the orphanage, her mother had been happy elsewhere giving her love to another man.

She was supporting her mother with money, but she was still angry at her. She had also enrolled Queen in Kisumu Medical Training College. Queen's son, Kelly, was being taken care of by their mother. Queen did not have to suffer for her mother's mistakes.

Gera had run away from her mother's house to go look for happiness, and she had found it in Brandon's arms, in his kisses, in his heart, and in his eyes.

She was so lost in her thoughts that she didn't even see him coming her way.

He tickled her, and she jumped with a start.

"Were you just thinking about me, darling?" he whispered in her ear.

"Actually, yes, and I think I need some private time with my husband," she replied boldly, and he did not need to be asked twice because he was already hot for her.

"Loiser, look after Gaya and Maya. We will be back in a few," he announced, and Loiser nodded.

They looked at each other lustfully for a while and were off their feet towards their hotel room. They had barely locked the door when they started tearing at each other's clothes. They made love like the first time, yet not quite like it, because nowadays, they knew the likes and dislikes of each other. But that did not prevent them from exploring new ways of doing it. Once they had finished, they held each other closely, feeling their heart beats.

It was less than ten minutes before he started raining more kisses on her and whispered, "I want to make more babies."

That alone sent her heart racing. Were the children all right? He saw the worried look in her face and got off the bed to look out for the children through the window, and she followed suit. Her stomach did a flip flop when she saw no sign of them. This already looked like déjà vu.

They quickly put on their clothes and went in search of them on the beach. They were nowhere to be seen. They asked people on the beach whether they had seen them, but nobody had.

"Calm down, Gera. We will find them," Brandon said, pulling her to his lap because she had been pacing for the past ten minutes.

"How can you be so sure? Maybe Ken has taken them."

"He is in prison, and he isn't getting out any time soon."

"Stop smiling. Maybe he escaped."

"Not a possibility."

She shook her head in disbelief. Why was life sometimes unfair to her?

Brandon held her close to him, and she wound her arms around his neck. She really needed an anchor. She would not be able to forgive herself if something happened to her children. She didn't even know how life was going to span without them. She didn't just want to live such a life.

***

Brandon was scared, but he knew that one person had to be strong for both of them. He loved his three children with the whole of his being. He dialled Loiser's number for the umpteenth time, but it went straight to the voice mail. He placed the phone on the table, distracted.

"Sweetie, please drink this," he told her after ordering a cold mango juice. She shook her head, but when he asked again, she sipped the drink.

"Sometimes, life is weird," she said, looking at the ocean.

"Why do you say that?"

"Just today, I was thinking of myself as a better mother than my mother."

"You are a better mother than most I know of."

"No, that's not true. We should have been out with them, Brandon. Maybe none of this would have happened."

"Worrying is like a rocking chair, my love. It gives you something to do, but it gets you nowhere," he said, rubbing her back soothingly.

They were still thinking of the children's possible destination when a Noah car parked a few meters from them. She quickly looked up, her heart beating faster. Brandon stood up from his seat expectantly.

The car door opened, and the three children rushed to their parents. Gera stood up from her seat, smiling while Brandon heaved a sigh of relief. He hugged Loiser tightly while the twins went to Gera. She held them close to her heart. She hadn't ever felt such profound love for all of them. Loiser went to her, hugging her closely.

Brandon looked at the car which had dropped the children, his hands in his pockets, and he walked forward. Whoever had taken the children had to be taught a lesson. Before he got nearer, the car door opened, and an old woman he didn't know got out. She was followed by Rosie and Clinton. He just wondered what the hell was happening.

Gera wanted to get up but she could not because Maya and Gaya had invaded her breasts hungrily. She caressed each of their heads as they suckled.

What was her mother doing here? She frowned as she looked their way.

Rosie whispered something to Brandon who then quickly glanced back at Gera. They walked back to her as Clinton and her mother stayed behind.

"What is it, honey?" she asked, looking from Brandon to Rosie.

"Let us take care of the children. You need to talk to your mother," Rosie said.

Gera still could not understand this.

"Has something happened to Queen or Kelly?" she asked impatiently.

"No, nothing like that," Rosie said, and she heaved a sigh of relief.

She finished breastfeeding Maya and Gaya and straightened her dress. Rosie and Brandon took the children, and they started moving towards the car.

"Don't do the disappearing act Rosie and Clinton staged a few minutes ago," she announced, waving at Clinton. They got into the car and drove away, leaving her and her mother staring at each other.

Her mother was standing a safe distance away. She looked very old and haggard, in a faded long Kitenge dress. Gera felt pity for her and motioned to the chair. She moved forward and sat on it. There was a tense silence for a while.

"How have you been?" her mother asked, trying to force a smile, and the wrinkles on her face intensified.

Gera was again reminded of how much her parent had aged.

"I'm fine," she said tersely and kept quiet.

"Listen, Gera, I am really sorry for the hurt I have caused you. I don't know how I can make it up to you. Please forgive me," she pleaded.

Gera looked at the beach. People were walking, couples were holding hands, and children were playing football.

"I now know better. I shouldn't have abandoned you at the orphanage. It was selfish of me to do that. I was only looking out for my best interest, and I am paying for it dearly. No mother should give up her responsibility of being a mother. I know I can't go back and right all the wrong, but I hope that with your forgiveness, maybe I can make up for the lost time," she continued, pleading for her understanding.

"You think that's enough. Let's just forget and forgive the past and open up a new chapter of our lives, right?" Gera shouted.

"Not really. I wish I could come up with concrete reasons to make you forgive me, but I have none. Please forgive me," her mother begged, going down on her knees, her eyes glittering with tears.

Gera remembered the day she had abandoned them at the orphanage, the way she always sat at the gate waiting, waiting, and waiting.

"You know the next day after you left, I went to the gate and waited for you. You had promised to come back for us. For months, I kept sitting by the gate waiting for you, but you never showed up," she said and felt tears trickle down her face. She angrily wiped them with the back of her hand.

"I am so sorry," her mother whispered, now crying.

"No, you are not sorry. You went and married that man and forgot about us," she said, getting angry.

They had been having a similar argument the day she'd left home. She was sick to the stomach of this. She could not take it anymore. She quickly stood up and started walking away.

"Gera, please don't leave. I don't want to lose you again," her mother pleaded.

You should have thought of that before you left us in the orphanage, she thought, trying to walk faster in the sand, but it was getting difficult.

"Gera, please ..." her mother called out.

She didn't know what particularly in that plea made her turn around. When she did, she saw her mother crawling on the sand to get to her, tears washing her face.

Something snapped in her. This wasn't fair. This wasn't helping either of them.

Unless you let go of the past hurt, you can never be truly happy—she recalled Mama Jane's words.

She walked back to where her mother was and helped her to her feet. She saw despair in her eyes. She hugged her and felt her mother tighten her hold on her.

It was like she was squeezing the tears of hurt out of Gera. She cried for about ten minutes, and her mother held her, consoling her. When she stopped crying, she didn't let go. Gera knew then that she wanted to be truly happy. This was all in the past. She had the present and the future.

She pulled back and said, "I forgive you."

Her mother's face lit up with a real smile this time, and she pulled Gera into a warm hug. It was then that Gera felt the gaping hole in her soul close up, and she was at peace with the world.

***

"What happened?" Brandon asked as they were resting on the porch.

He was sipping beer while she had opted for a Coke. He couldn't shake the feeling that something had changed in her. He couldn't put a finger to it. Her eyes were brighter, her skin was glowing, and she was more beautiful tonight than he had ever seen her. He was again transported to that day he had seen her on the swings in the orphanage. He could not believe that this amazing woman was his to share the rest of his life with.

"I forgave my mother," she said, looking at him.

"Are you sure, my love?" he asked, pulling her onto his lap. She nodded, and he kissed her all over the face. "So does that mean that I will finally meet my mother-in-law officially to give her dowry?"

"Get your suit ready," she said, smiling.

He held her in his arms, and although he had told her a thousand times how much he loved her, he knew with certainty that he had never been overwhelmed with the feeling as he was tonight.

"It's the night of the full moon," she noted, pointing at the sky.

"What's with the full moon?" he asked, smiling.

"The first time you kissed me, it was the night of the full moon."

"Ooh. I want to relive that night, but tonight, I want kiss every inch of your body all night long," he whispered, and she shivered in anticipation.

He carried her to their bedroom and made love to her with his body, heart, and soul. When it was all over, they cuddled close.

In the candlelight, Gera looked into his eyes, and she saw that place called happiness.

THE END

Thank you for reading A Place Called Happiness by Diana Anyango. If you enjoyed this story, please leave a review on the site of purchase.

Ever since Diana Anyango read Nicholas Sparks' 'Message in a Bottle' after completing Class 8, she has been an avid romance reader. When she got to Form 3, she started visualizing her own characters and decided to put pen to paper. The journey has been long and tough but she believed in her characters and knew that one day she would share them with the world.

Connect with Diana
Facebook: facebook.com/diana.silvia.967
Twitter: twitter.com/DianaAnyango18
Instagram: instagram.com/dianasilviaanyango/
Blog: princessdeedotcom.wordpress.com/

OTHER BOOKS BY LOVE AFRICA PRESS

Not Just Another Interlude by Lara T Kareem
Fine Maple by Emem Bassey
A Little Bit of Love's Magic by Bambo Deen
One More Night by Rosemary Okafor

CONNECT WITH US

Facebook.com/LoveAfricaPress
Twitter.com/LoveAfricaPress
Instagram.com/LoveAfricaPress

SIGN UP TO OUR NEWSLETTER
https://www.loveafricapress.com/newsletter

www.ingramcontent.com/pod-product-compliance
Lightning Source LLC
Chambersburg PA
CBHW061447210726
48287CB00007B/2400